I would like to say thank you to all you lovely readers for reading this book, I am overwhelmed that you enjoy the stories I'm telling.

Thank you to my family for supplying the many women in my life growing up that gave the inspiration for these characters.

My final big thank you is to my wife, editor-in-chief and murder researcher (I'm sorry if you end up on some watch list) Laura I couldn't and wouldn't have had the courage to do this without you supporting me. It means more to me than I can say. Thank you and I love you xx

CHAPTER 1

◆ ◆ ◆

DCI Ellie McVey was sprinting down West George Street fast on the heels of Tony McDaid, the man she had been investigating for heroin dealing for the past 2 months.

"Tony Stop! You're just making this harder for yourself" she shouted at the back of his head as she dodged pedestrians, gaining ground on him inch by inch.

"Get to fuck ya cow" was the witty retort back. He ran across Renfield Street, narrowly missing a bus which Ellie had to wait on passing. She knew it was only a matter of time before she got to him, Tony was not known for his athletic prowess. He was on at least 40 a day and spent most of his day at the pub.

"Tony! I can't be arsed chasing you all over the town! You know full well I'll outrun you so just stop pissing about and then we can get to the station without needing an iron lung for you!" she bellowed.

She was gaining on him again when, out of nowhere, an old man rugby tackled Tony and wrestled him to the ground. Ellie skidded to a halt beside the pair and immediately cuffed Tony, who was very compliant now that he was in a headlock and winded from the tackle.

"Thanks for that" Ellie said to the old man.

"Just doing my duty, I'm a retired constable. It felt good to be tackling someone again" his eyes were lit up with pure joy and excitement, still using the headlock.

"You can release him now Sir, I think he is turning blue." Ellie warned as she hauled Tony to his feet now that he was able to breathe again.

"Mental old bastard, you coulda killed both of us" grumbled Tony.

"Tony you've just been taken down by a pensioner. If you don't want that spread about to all your pals then I suggest you shut it" Ellie whispered to him as she hauled him round and called for DS Bickerton to bring the car.

Gavin Bickerton, her partner, arrived a few moments later and pulled the car up to the kerb. He grinned as he unceremoniously bundled Tony into the back of the car "I knew you would be better chasing him than I would"

"Only because you've had chippy dinners every night this week, the sooner your wife gets back the better" she quipped as she got into the passenger seat. "When is she back by the way?"

"Tomorrow, so I better get the house cleaned tonight or she will kill me. It looks like a right tip"

"Nooo really?" joked Ellie.

"Shut up, you can always come around and help me" he batted his eyelashes at her.

"No chance, I'm knackered. Besides, it was my turn to clean and cook last night at home."

"Aww bless, can't believe she's finally got you all domesticated" laughed Gavin.

"It looks like it" said Ellie also laughing.

She would never have thought that her life would have become so settled. Since she met Kate nearly a year ago, her life has been turned upside down. They had moved in together a few months ago and had settled into domestic bliss. Kate was a writer and had just finished her latest novel. The publisher had hopes of it reaching the bestseller chart and Ellie couldn't be more proud of her. She was looking forward to getting home, it had been a long day.

"Bruiser! Put that down!" Kate glared at the shih tzu puppy who was currently chewing her slipper. He spat it out and gave her his best doggy grin before he ran off in search of his protector, Bella the Westie. Kate couldn't help but smile, he was too cute to be angry with. She picked up her soggy slipper and some other clothes and put them through to the bedroom. She was trying to make the place a bit tidier for Ellie coming home. She had been trying to think of a plot for a new book but her creative process meant that she had spread crumpled paper and crisp packets all over the place. Ellie had been working hard recently on trying to catch some major drug dealers, Kate figured she could at least make her evenings a little easier.

Kate had just finished setting the plates for dinner when Ellie came through the door. She groaned and walked zombie like to the couch and collapsed into it with a happy sigh. Kate watched her antics with amusement from the doorway.

"Hard day honey?" she asked as she walked round and sat on the edge of the couch.

"Oh yeah, but a productive one. We got Tony McDaid"

"That's great, well done! I know how much work you and Gavin have put into that investigation. Come on, I've made dinner, you can tell me all about it." She pulled Ellie up and led her by the hand to the kitchen.

"Well you remember how we got a tip that McDaid had been seen talking in the pub with Jamie Smith the local dealer for Maryhill?" said Ellie as she sat down to a dinner of pasta.

"Yes, that barmaid that took a shine to Gavin called you with the information?" asked Kate as she put down some warm French bread.

"Carol? Yes that's right, so she called again this morning to say that McDaid was back in and had handed a package over to Jamie and that Jamie had handed over a thick envelope. She told us that they were still there having a drink, so we got in the car and headed to the pub. We burst in and caught them in the act; uniform grabbed Jamie and the package of drugs but McDaid legged it out the fire exit so I had to chase him down."

"Well done, see I knew that once you started jogging it would be useful" joked Kate

"Well actually no, that's the best bit! I didn't catch him, an old boy that was coming out of the sushi place off Renfield Street tackled him! He must have been well in his 70s" said Ellie as Kate laughed at the image.

"Have you charged him?" asked Kate as her laughter died down
"Yes, we've charged him with drug trafficking and distribution. The pub CCTV clearly shows the handover. We caught them with £1.5 million worth of heroin and over £90,000 in cash. The CPS are going through the evidence right now and Jamie is grassing in everyone he knows that's involved so that he gets a reduced sentence."

"Ah I'm glad that it's finally over, you've been on that case for so long. Congratulations honey" smiled Kate as she raised her glass in a toast.

They were half way through their pasta when the front door

burst open. Aunt Peggy rushed in to the kitchen excitedly and plonked herself down at the table.

"Girls I have news, we are all going on holiday next week!"

"What?...How?..." stuttered Kate.

"Both excellent questions, Peggy explain" said Ellie through a mouthful of pasta.

"Well, you know how I love listening to the local radio when I'm at work?"
When they both shrugged their shoulders she continued. "They had a competition, it was to guess all the songs and the highest correct score wins. I called up and I won! The prize is a ten day cruise for four around the Western Mediterranean. We leave next Tuesday!"

"Really? That's great! Congratulations Aunt Peggy" Kate jumped up and hugged her followed by Ellie.

"I know, I can't wait, your mum is already trying to pack. Ellie you will get time off won't you?" She asked hopefully.

"I don't see why not, I've just finished a case I've been working on. I think I am due a little holiday" Ellie grinned.

"Well that's sorted then, we're off to the Med!"

CHAPTER 2

◆ ◆ ◆

T he week passed in a flurry of activity, Kate was packing while Ellie finished up the paperwork for all her cases ready for trial. Gavin had been more than happy to take Bella and Bruiser to his house while they would be away; his wife loved dogs and was looking forward to having them.

Ellie returned home and dumped her briefcase in the hall. She heard voices in the living room; she found Kate and Aggie in the living room huddled over a laptop.

"What are you two up to?" Ellie asked as she kissed Kate and then gave Aggie a hug. She dropped down beside them on the couch to see what they were looking at.

"We're looking at the trips and excursions we can book for the cruise. There's loads of them." said Aggie as she scrolled through the options.

"Ellie there's a trip to Pompeii!" Kate said full of excitement "I've always wanted to see it"

"Well that's the first one to book honey, what else have we got?" Ellie said smiling at Kate's enthusiasm

"There's a trip in Sicily to an ancient temple and a bus tour of

Rome which would be good for me in case the fatigue kills me." Said Kate

"They've got loads of vineyard tours and even a gin tour Ellie, oh Peggy will love that." Aggie exclaimed as she clicked on the website to book every wine tour."

Kate was a bit apprehensive about that; she had a feeling that chaos would be on the cards.

"Mum I'm warning you right now, I know what you two are like after a few drinks. If we have to apologise for you or bail you out in every port we come to, so help me….I'll tell gran" Kate glared at Aggie.

"Bit harsh love, there's no need to drag her into this. Peggy and I are adults, I don't see how you can think we would embarrass ourselves in that manner" sniffed Aggie folding her arms in a huff.

Glasgow airport was full to the brim with holidaymakers all wandering around trying to find the correct check-in desks. There was a huge queue for the airline taking them to Palma where they would meet their ship. After standing for a little while, Kate started to get a bit tired. She had been so busy trying to get ready for the cruise that it had drained her of her energy.

"Honey, do you want to go find a seat until we get closer to the desk? I can keep our luggage here with me." Ellie offered, noticing Kate's exhaustion.

"What's wrong, Kate are you starting to tire?" Peggy asked. "I'll see to this, give me one minute" and with that Peggy disappeared towards the front of the queue. They didn't have to wait long before she arrived back dragging a terrified young man by the elbow.

"Now Lewis, this is my niece. As I was telling you, she has M.S. and standing in this queue is not good for her, so I suggest you find a way to hurry this process up"

"B...but ma'am there's nothing I can do about the queue I..." he stammered

"Yes yes you said all that before, I really wish you wouldn't repeat yourself young man" said Peggy impatiently "Now either get us to a quicker queue or I shall be in contact with my good friend Eric Parsons about this." Lewis went pale and instantly escorted them towards the special assistance queue. He practically ran away as soon as he could.

"Peggy what did you do to that poor boy?" demanded Aggie as she slapped her sisters arm.

"Nothing, I just threatened him with the CEO of the airport, Eric and I go way back" Peggy shrugged.

"I can't believe you did that to him, he looked terrified." Ellie was holding in laughter, she coughed a little and got double glares from Aggie and Kate. She promptly stopped laughing and whispered to Peggy "you are so on your own with this one."

"Coward" was the whispered response back.

The queue was considerably shorter, in fact there were only a few people ahead of them. There was a family with a child with the autism awareness lanyard around her neck and an elderly couple, the wife holding on to a walker.

"Out of my way please!" Came the order behind them. An older woman was behind them in a Motability scooter waving her arms to get them to move.

"There's a queue here love" responded Aggie coolly.

"Yes I can see that, but I don't need to queue." The woman said snootily and without another word she motored up to the beginning of the queue almost mowing down the woman with the walker as she went. She was followed by another woman carrying cases.

"Have you ever seen the like?!" Peggy exclaimed. "I've a good mind to drag her out of that scooter and.."

"Aunt Peggy calm down, you can hardly mouth off at her considering what you've just done to poor Lewis." Said Kate.

"That was different, I was getting you the help that you needed. She was just being a rude obnoxious old b.."

"Yes we get it but there's no need for her to spoil the start of our holiday Peggy dear, now give it a rest" Aggie said putting an end to things.

They got checked in soon after this and headed towards the sky lounge where they could rest up in comfort before their flight. Ellie got coffees for herself and Kate and wine for Aggie and Peggy. They had settled into a comfortable silence when they heard commotion coming from the entrance to the lounge. They saw a tall older gentleman with a white moustache and a red face arguing with the concierge.

"Listen to me my good woman, I booked into the sky lounge last week. I've lost that ridiculous scrap of paper I was given as a receipt but if you would bother to look at that computer in front of you, you will see my name. Major Edward Charleston, be a good girl and check it."

"What a blustering buffoon" muttered Peggy, Ellie nodded in agreement. She looked at him, he was military through and through. His blazer buttons were gleaming and his shoes smartly polished. His grey hair was in a neat short back and sides and even his moustache looked combed. He had the complexion of a man who enjoyed a drink, ruddy and a little sweaty. The poor concierge finally found his name on the computer and issued him with his ticket for the lounge. He didn't even thank her, just barged past and headed for the bar.

"You meet such delightful people when you travel" said Ellie "I hope he's not going on the cruise, he doesn't seem to be with anyone."

They were informed by the tannoy that due to bad weather in Palma, their flight was delayed by two hours. Their time passed happily enough though as they played cards (Peggy won a fortune at Texas hold'em) and soon their flight was called for boarding. When they arrived at the gate Ellie noticed that the Major was indeed going to be on their flight. They were queued up for boarding, Kate had been moved to the special assistance queue again as they had spotted her walking stick. As they neared to front of the queue they heard a familiar voice.

"Can you let me past please, you're in my way"

"I don't believe it, tell me that old cow is not doing this again" growled Peggy as she turned to find her nemesis in the scooter behind them once more. Yet again she manoeuvred round them and reached the head of the queue flashing her passport and ticket at the attendant.

"I didn't think the Queen and the Queen Mother needed passports when they travelled. It must just be when they are slumming it with the rest of us plebs" Peggy said in her loudest voice. The Queen turned round in her scooter seat, looked Peggy up and down and then set off towards the plane with the Queen Mother in tow.

They finally got boarded and settled in to their seats. Aggie and Peggy were sat in the row in front of them. A young woman sat in the aisle seat beside Ellie, she introduced herself as Jen before settling herself in front of her phone. There was then an announcement from the cabin crew.

"Good afternoon ladies and gentlemen, my name is Stacey and I'm your cabin crew supervisor on this Scotia-air flight from Glasgow to Palma. Your crew today will be Aaron, Melanie and

Danielle. We would like to apologise for the delay to this flight, we are currently trying to refuel as quickly as possible and have you on your way. Before we commence the safety demonstration I would like to announce that, due to a passenger allergy, we will not be serving any snacks that contain nuts on this flight. Can I please request that if you have brought any items on board that may contain nuts, that you please keep them stored in your luggage until you leave the plane. We thank you for your assistance in this matter. We are cleared for take-off so I'm going to hand you over to Danielle for the safety announcement. I hope you enjoy your flight."

Half way through the flight Kate woke up from a short sleep. "Honey I'm a bit worried, we had a delay before the flight left. What if the ship leaves without us? It's supposed to leave at 6pm but I don't think we will land until at least 6.30."

Ellie was about to respond when Jen answered for her.

"Is it the Dreamliner cruise you are talking about? Don't worry, they don't leave without all flights coming in. They will have been alerted to the delay. I'm going out to work on the ship so I know it won't leave." Jen smiled in assurance.

Kate smiled in relief "Thank you, I was worried. Do you like working on the ship?"

"I don't know yet, it's my first day. I've worked on other liners for the company though so I know it will be fun. You will have a great time, I promise" Jen smiled.

They arrived at Palma airport just before 6.30pm and boarded coaches that would take them to the ship. It was a short journey and soon the ship came into view. It was a hotel on water; that was the best way Ellie could describe it. The large white ship was bustling with passengers and staff carrying suitcases. Once they were off the coach they queued up at the terminal for passport control and to receive their keys and boarding cards.

"I don't believe it, will you look at this" growled Peggy as she watched the Queen get pushed in a wheelchair up to the front of the queue yet again.

"What's happened to her scooter?" said Aggie as she held Peggy's sleeve to prevent her marching up and throttling the woman.

"They've probably had to take it on board for her. Peggy you need to calm down, you will be spending the next ten days with her. At this rate you will be pitching her over the side before we even reach Italy." Kate warned. The queue moved on and they finally got their keys before they made their way to the gang-way entrance to the ship. Peggy was still muttering dark curses under her breath.

They finally got to their room on deck 5, Kate slumped grate-fully onto the couch on the left of the cabin. It was a tidy room, the bed had crisp white sheets and their towels had been folded into beautiful swans. There was a small bathroom, wardrobes, a mini bar and a flat screen tv mounted to the wall. There was a note on the dresser to introduce their cabin steward Eduardo and a booklet called 'Cruise News' that detailed all the events happening on board for the next day. It would be a day at sea so they could explore the ship and relax after the stress of today.

Ellie unpacked as Kate slept, her fatigue taking its toll on her. They had agreed to meet Aggie and Peggy at their cabin on deck 8 as there was a buffet restaurant close to their cabin. An hour later, Ellie woke Kate and they freshened up for dinner. They collected Aggie and Peggy and headed to the buffet. It was quiet as most passengers had already eaten and were now enjoying the various entertainments the ship had to offer. They took a table out on the lido deck and enjoyed their meals. The barman brought over rum punches which Peggy gleefully accepted. The ship had set sail and they watched the twinkling lights of Palma in the distance.

"Here's to a wonderful holiday ladies" toasted Aggie as they finished their drinks. They headed to their cabins exhausted from the day and ready to start fresh in the morning.

CHAPTER 3

◆ ◆ ◆

Ellie and Kate slept like the dead. They didn't even notice the sway of the ship during the night. Kate woke fresh and happy, she rolled over to cuddle in to Ellie's back placing a soft kiss on her shoulder.

"Morning" mumbled Ellie still half asleep as she enjoyed the gentle touch.

"Morning honey, did you sleep well?" whispered Kate as she continued to kiss Ellie's shoulder.

"Mmm, I didn't think I would sleep so well if I'm honest." Ellie rolled over to face Kate, she kissed her sweetly and pressed their foreheads together. "You ready to go exploring? Take a notebook with you, I have a feeling this ship will be a gold mine for characters" she grinned. Kate laughed and admitted that she had brought a notebook, just in case.

"Well come on then, let's see what this place is all about eh?" Ellie jumped out of bed, pulling Kate gently up to her. She kissed her lovingly and then pulled her towards the shower.

"These aren't built for two you know?" said Kate as she was led by the hand into the bathroom. Ellie winked as she said "Wanna bet?"

At breakfast they were eating French toast and coffee when they were joined by Aggie carrying a bowl of porridge and a cup of tea.

"Where's Peggy got to?" asked Kate as she scanned the room. Aggie gave her a look.

"She is still piling her plate. I left her at the bacon stage of the process. I'm telling you, watching Peggy at a buffet is like watching an art and architecture exhibition all in one. Oh here she comes, will you look at that plate." Peggy was gingerly making her way to the table with a mountain of fried food on her plate. As she sat down they noticed 6 sausages, a mound of bacon, what must have been a full tin of beans, 3 fried eggs and 4 hash browns. Her backside had barely touched her seat when she sprang back up. "I forgot my toast". She was back minutes later with 4 rounds of toast.

"Peggy you are going to drop of a heart attack one of these days. You won't be fit for anything but your bed after eating all that" scolded Aggie.

"Aggie dear get off my case, I have been eating a fried breakfast for most of my life and look at me, a picture of health. The body and brain need fuelling. There's pub quizzes on this ship at night. I need my brain food." At that Peggy started to heap bacon and beans into her mouth with a happy moan.

"Well don't come running to me if you drop dead" muttered Aggie as she toyed with her congealing porridge. She pushed it away and sighed. "Oh give me a sausage woman, I'm starving". Peggy smirked as she pushed a sausage and some bacon onto her toast plate and passed it to Aggie. Ellie heard Peggy triumphantly whisper "one-nil".

They walked along the corridors after breakfast and after a

while Kate noticed something about the artwork that was hanging on the corridor walls. She nudged Ellie "Have you noticed the theme of the art around here?" Ellie looked at the pictures. They were all nudes, female and male nudes in various poses. "They're um....different" Kate commented.

"I think Peggy has booked us on a saga swingers cruise honey. I'm convinced of it." Ellie muttered, Kate nodded her head in agreement. They went out on deck to take in the view, there was a man looking pale and grey. He was hugging the rail and groaning. Aggie went over to him and touched his shoulder.

"Are you alright dear?" she asked him.

"That depends, do you know a cure for seasickness?" he groaned pitifully. Peggy decided she would answer his question.

"Yes young man, I know the perfect cure for seasickness. Sit under a tree." She walked away leaving him staring at her in disbelief.

"Sit under a tree she says. Sit under a tree, why didn't I bloody think of that!" he turned and retched over the railing.

"Peggy you're pure evil" laughed Ellie.

They explored the many restaurants on each deck, they found the theatre and noticed it had an Abba tribute show on that night. The bars were all full of passengers making use of the all-inclusive drinks package. At the pool bar there was a free table and they decided to have a seat and a drink to enjoy the sun. Beside the pool there was a holiday rep dressed in crisp white shorts with a microphone and an 'organised fun' clipboard.

"Good afternoon ladies and gentlemen. I'm Michelle and I'm here to tell you of all the fun things we have planned for you on board today. At 1.15pm we have a lawn bowling tournament on deck 7 so anyone who would like to take part can pop along and see Nadine who will set you up with everything you need.

At 2.30pm in the mermaid club we have ballroom dancing lessons with Destiny and Manuel so get your dancing shoes on and get a seven from Len! At 4.00pm we have a bridge tournament in the card room on deck 9 and then our evening entertainment begins. There is an ABBA tribute in the Boardwalk Theatre, cabaret begins at 7pm in the show lounge and in the mermaid club we have a pub quiz and the topic is music through the decades which begins at 8.30pm. We hope to see you all there."

Kate and Ellie had listened to all of this with amusement. "Bowls and ballroom dancing, honey we are on the good ship cocoon" whispered Kate as Ellie snorted into her drink.

"No, it's more like 'Hi-De-Hi' hello campers stuff. All that's missing is the tannoy announcements about knobbly knees competitions" joked Ellie. No sooner had she finished saying that, a crackling sound was heard followed by a few bongs on a xylophone. There were speakers situated all over the ship and now there was a voice emanating from them.

"Good afternoon everyone this is the voice from the ceiling" crackled the tannoy.

"You are kidding" said Ellie incredulously "It is bloody 'Hi-De-Hi" we're going to be singing goodnight campers at night and watching glamourous gran competitions! I'm going to kill Peggy if that happens"

CHAPTER 4

◆ ◆ ◆

After further exploration on the outside decks they found some sun loungers by the pool and relaxed in the sunshine. Aggie was sleeping off her rum punch, Peggy was working her way through the GCHQ puzzle book; actually she was laughing and correcting the errors she found in it. Kate was making notes for her new book and watching the people that walked past. Ellie was people watching from behind her sunglasses. It was an occupational hazard that was difficult to switch off.

The ship had a strange mix of characters she thought. She settled on watching a couple sitting on top of the life jacket trunk to the left of them, it was tucked away in a corner. They weren't dressed like your average holiday maker. They were dressed in black combat trousers and heavy duty boots, they had a blueprint map spread between them and they were speaking in urgent whispers. "No, no that won't work at all, we need clear access. I think we should use this." Ellie heard that their accent was American. That was unusual enough to perk her interest, it was rare for non-British people to be on a British cruise ship. She got up and moved closer to them on the pretence of looking at the view from the railing, she wanted to hear more of their conversation.

"What if we double back this way and then access this area here....?" said the man of the couple

"No it will be too busy, if we go this way it should be quiet at that time..." the woman replied as she pointed to something on the map. They halted their conversation abruptly when they spotted Ellie. They rolled up the map they had been studying and went back inside the ship without a backward glance but not before Ellie had managed to look at the map. It was a blue-print of one of the decks of the ship. She walked back to her sun-lounger deep in thought.

"What's wrong honey? You look thoughtful" asked Kate as Ellie dropped down behind her on her sun lounger and pulled her into an embrace.

"Oh, nothing...I was just watching that couple and they've got me thinking that's all. They were acting weird" explained Ellie.

"Why have they got you concerned? That...." Kate, turning in Ellie's arms, pointed at her frown "Is your concerned face."

"They were just....I don't know....odd, out of place. I mean who wears combat trousers and boots on a cruise ship? Why are Americans on this cruise anyway? They have loads of cruise ships that are massive so why chose this one? Why were they studying a deck map as if their lives depended on it?" Ellie rhymed off the questions rolling about in her head.

"They could be trying to find their way around this place, it all looks the same and I've already got lost a couple of times" suggested Aggie opening one eye.

"Yeah..maybe.." agreed Ellie, but she was still deep in thought. They bothered her and she couldn't put her finger on why. Kate leaned over and kissed her cheek.

"You need to switch that big brain off for a while, you're on holiday. You need to stop looking for criminals lurking around every corner" teased Kate as she turned back and pulled Ellie's arms around her waist. Ellie laughed as she cuddled closer and relaxed.

"You're right, I'll relax I promise" she kissed the top of Kate's head and settled back.

A couple arrived not long after this and settled themselves in the loungers beside Peggy. They were in their 50's, the husband was overweight with ruddy cheeks and dark hair. The wife was a short woman with a kind face and greying hair. They were both dressed in tan coloured shorts and matching sandals.

"Oh doing a puzzle book are you? My wife loves them, is it a good one?" the man said to Peggy.

"Yes, it's a challenging one so I'm enjoying it immensely". Peggy responded.

"I'm Peter and this is the wife, Rose and you lovely ladies are?"

"I'm Peggy, this is my sister Aggie, my niece Kate and her partner Ellie." Peter shook each of their hands warmly.

"Pleasure to meet you all, is this your first time on the cruise?" asked Rose.

"Yes; it's a new experience for us, have you been before?" asked Aggie as she sat up to talk to the newcomers properly.

"Oh yes we're old hands, been on this particular ship over six times now. The staff are all marvellous, very friendly people. If we were to give you some advice it would be to fill bottles of water at the fountains on decks 5 and 7, the mini bar charges a small fortune for bottled water and you'll be needing it to boil the kettle for tea. If you are going to be doing the pub quizzes get there early, the lounge fills with coffin dodgers quickly so you will be lucky to get a seat after 8pm." As Peter mentioned coffin dodgers Ellie laughed but quickly covered it with a cough.

"Thank you for the advice, we will definitely fill the water bottles at the fountains. Are you planning on taking in any of the excursions? I suppose if you've been on this cruise so many times you may have seen everything already" said Aggie.

"Oh no, the ship does several different cruises, I think we've only done this particular one a couple of times so there's still plenty to see. We are doing wine tasting in Toulon, the gin tour in Genoa and we are going back to Pompeii again. Are you fine ladies going on any trips?" said Derek with a smile, he had leaned forward on his lounger and full of attention.

"Yes Peggy and I are doing the wine tasting and the gin tour too but the girls are doing sightseeing instead as they aren't big drinkers. We are all doing Pompeii though as well as Rome and Sicily so we have a full holiday of trips." Aggie explained.

"We will have to meet up then, keep each other company. I couldn't forgive myself if I let such beauties as you go into these countries unchaperoned." Peter said gallantly, or at least that's how he had intended to sound but to look at Peggy's reaction, this did not go down well at all.

"We are perfectly capable of travelling without the need of a man on our arms. We thank you for the invitation but we will be perfectly safe on our own" she put her book back in her bag and go up to leave. Aggie whispered an apology to Rose explaining that Peggy was fiercely independent.

"Oh no need to apologise, he forgets that it's not 1922. Hopefully we will see you at the quiz later" Rose smiled as they all go up and trooped off after Peggy.

CHAPTER 5

◆ ◆ ◆

Ellie was getting dressed for dinner as Kate was in the shower. They had caught up with Peggy earlier and managed to calm her down once she had a feminist rant about Peter. Once she got it all out of her system she returned to her calm self once more and was looking forward to 'decimating these old gits at the music quiz'. Ellie was putting her watch on when she heard raised voices outside. She went to the door and quietly opened it just enough to peek outside to see what was going on. She heard a loud male voice.

"What's done is done, there's nothing I can do it about it now so just leave me alone!"

She peeked out and saw that it was the Major but couldn't see who he was talking to. The other person had hushed their tone to a whisper. Ellie thought it could be a woman's voice but couldn't be 100% sure, but definitely heard them as they harshly whispered

"You'll pay you bastard; I've waited far too long for this moment. It's time."

Other voices could now be heard coming down the corridor from the other direction. The Major turned away and walked past Ellie's hastily closing door. The other person did not follow him past the door, Ellie peeked back out but there was a throng of people now walking in the corridor on their way to dinner, whoever had threatened the Major was gone.

When she closed the door again, Kate exited the bathroom fresh from her shower. She sat down at the dresser to brush her hair and looked at Ellie in the mirror. She watched her for a few moments and then turned round.

"Ellie, you're pacing. What's happened?"

"Hmm? Oh nothing. I just overheard an argument outside that sounded serious. Someone threatened the Major, I don't know who it was though."

"Threatened him? What with?" Kate looked concerned and she sat quietly as Ellie told her of the whispered conversation that she had overheard. Kate continued to look thoughtful after Ellie had finished and then Kate got up and started pacing too. Ellie laughed

"Pacing appears to be contagious."

Kate stopped mid pace and resumed getting dressed, she looked back at Ellie and asked "How concerned are you about this honey?"

"Honestly? I'm not sure. I don't know the context of the conversation but it was troubling. Hopefully it's nothing but a row over a game of poker or something and I'm just reading too much into it. Come on; let's go meet the family for dinner." Kate finished getting dressed, applied some perfume and they left the room.

Aggie and Peggy had secured a table in the restaurant so Kate and Ellie queued up for the buffet. Ellie was waiting for the carvery turkey and noticed that she was behind the Major. He was moving slowly along the buffet choices asking the servers what was in each dish. He moved away from the Chinese stir fry and the chicken satay skewers and finally opted for the fish and chips option much to the relief of the servers. He moved off towards the drinks station and Ellie got to the carvery just in time to hear the servers say

"What is it with him? Every meal he's had he always asks what's in the dish, he's driving me crazy. At breakfast he did the same thing with every single pastry on offer and then what did he do? He had cornflakes!" They noticed Ellie and ended the conversation and served her the turkey with a smile. When she got to the table she told Aggie and Peggy about the argument she had heard outside her door and the Major's unusual behaviour at the buffet.

"He might be a fussy eater; I know that Kate has trouble getting sandwiches in meal deals because she can't eat mayonnaise. Maybe he is just particular?" explained Aggie sensibly.

"Yeah that's a good point, I forgot about Kate's sandwich dilemmas"

"He might also been one of those people that doesn't eat foreign food. There are plenty of people his age that live on fish suppers, roast beef and mince and tatties." said Peggy as she cut up her steak. "The argument is unusual though, I mean who gets into a row on the first full day of their holiday? It must be someone who he already knew" she said reasonably.

"He's here on his own isn't he? I don't remember him with anyone on the journey do you?" asked Kate, they all shook their heads. As far as they could remember, the Major travelled by himself and hadn't met up with anyone that they could see. They finished their meal and Peggy had them all up and ready for the quiz. They headed towards the lounge to get a table early, as recommended by their new friends Peter and Rose.

When they arrived at the lounge it was already starting to fill up even though the quiz wouldn't be starting for another hour. They found a table along the side by the windows. They had no sooner sat down than Aggie had nabbed a waiter and procured rum punches for the table and some soft drinks for Kate and Ellie. Peggy was already in the zone, she was scanning the tables to suss out her competition. The queen and the queen mother were sat at the front with several glasses in front of them. They were pointing and glaring at two men beside them. The men were dressed in loud Hawaiian style shirts and had matching handlebar moustaches. They were laughing as they drank wine and the younger of the two leaned in for a kiss. They seemed very much in love and Peggy watched them with a smile. She noticed that when the couple were kissing, the Queen's face contorted in disgust and Peggy instantly felt rage. She hated such narrow-mindedness, she had always been fiercely protective of Kate against such treatment. She would never admit it, but when she found out that a girl at school had been picking on Kate for being gay, she got a friend from work to go 'have a word' with the girl. She never went near Kate after that.

The Major was sitting at a table at the back with a bottle of red wine in front of him and gesturing animatedly to the people at the next table. Peter and Rose were at the other side of the lounge with another couple looking relaxed. The lounge was now pretty full, there was a group singing old classics on stage, they weren't bad at all and Peggy started humming along to a Dusty Springfield number as Aggie called for the waiter again for more rum punch.

The band finished their number and got a polite round of applause. As they left the stage a man in a white tuxedo jacket bounded up the steps and grabbed a microphone. He was spray tanned to a David Dickinson shade of mahogany and his teeth were a dazzling white. He introduced himself as Dave the entertainment host on board the ship and did the usual pleasantries of hoping everyone was having a good time. There was a quiet giggled "Hi-De-Hi" from a now tipsy Aggie as Dave was running through the entertainment for the evening.

"Ok ladies and gents its quiz time, todays quiz is music through the decades. You should all have answer sheets in front of you; all you have to do is write down the song and the artist from the clip of music that we play. Easy enough? Right we'll kick off then shall we? Here comes your first question"

A song was played that Ellie didn't recognise but Kate grabbed the paper off Peggy and jotted down an answer. Ellie looked at it and then turned back to Kate "Really? You got B*Witched that quickly huh? And it's not even that wee Irish dancing song. Who are you?" she teased as Kate gave her a subtle hand gesture while scratching her nose.

The next song was tough, both Ellie and Peggy recognised it but couldn't think of the name of the song. Ellie was trying to hum the tune to herself, hoping she could get to the chorus and remember the name. This was hindered by Aggie, now on her fourth rum punch, who was singing Abba's Fernando to herself.

"Not helping Aggie dear" said Peggy through clenched teeth. They had to move on from that song. The next one Ellie got quickly and wrote down 'Eye of the Tiger' by survivor "it was number one when I was born" she explained to Peggy.

The next one Peggy knew was by Elvis. Aggie however, had decided it was Hey Jude by the Beatles and was singing it while trying to wrestle the pen away from Peggy to write it down. They weren't doing great. Between Peggy and Kate, they managed to get a Take That song, Guns and roses and Dr Dre 'No diggity.' Peggy got that one to the amazement of all.

By the end of the quiz they knew they had no chance of winning, Aggie was now trying to eat a packet of crisps with one eye open but only succeeded in crunching crumbs all over the place. Kate moved the latest rum punch away from her mother quickly.

It's time to mark the quiz, Dave started to ask the audience the answers rather than announcing them. There was a man at a table in the middle of the room that shouted out not only every song and artist but also the month and year they were released. Peggy's eye was twitching, Kate knew that was a bad sign. After a few more answers were shouted out by this man, Peggy had obviously had enough

"Aye we could all have cheated and used Shazam ya cheeky wee bast..." the rest of the rant was curtailed by Kate digging her aunt in the ribs. Peggy glared at her but remained silent, although she continued to stare daggers at her new nemesis at the table in front.

Dave was back as all the scores had been totalled and there were three teams tied for the win.

"Can I ask one member from each team to join me on stage, we are going to have a sing off for the win! Come on up now folks, the prize for the winner is a collector's edition Dream Liner beach towel" The crowd went a bit pantomime at this point and dutifully cheered and 'oooo'ed' at the magnificent prize up for grabs.

The three delegates from the winning teams had made it on stage, Peggy growled as she spotted her nemesis was among them. Ellie heard a petulant grumble of 'cheaters never prosper' from her and she hid her smile and turned back to the stage.

"Now the rules are simple, you each get to choose a song from the list and then you perform that song. Best performance will win the prize. First cab off the rank is Rhonda and where are you from my love?"

"Belfast" this got a small cheer from the crowd.

"Ok Rhonda love, what song have you chosen to sing?"

"Madonna, Like a Virgin" another cheer went up.

"Tonight ladies and gents for one night only, Rhonda from Belfast is Madonna!" Dave announced as Rhonda took centre stage and the opening bars of the track started. It wasn't a bad performance, she sang all the right lyrics and did a few little gyrations around the stage and when it was finished she got a healthy round of applause.

"Well done Rhonda love, that was brilliant. Next contestant is Andy, where are you from Andy?"

"W..Wigan" he whispered but few people heard him to cheer. Andy was a tiny man with an even smaller voice. He looked terrified but Dave didn't appear to notice.

"Andy, what's your song choice? You've a lot to live up to after Rhonda's stellar performance." This didn't help, Andy went pale and Ellie honestly thought he was ready to pass out.

"I'm doing 'Your song' by Elton John" he whispered. Dave didn't give him a chance to change his mind, he quickly announced the song louder so that people could hear and then scarpered off stage leaving Andy trembling alone. As soon as the piano keys could be heard, Andy seemed to gain a little confidence and started to sing. He had a pretty good voice and, although not a great performance, he sang the song beautifully. He also got a healthy applause from the audience. He seemed to grow six inches taller with the adulation and had to actually be shepherded off the stage by Dave.

"And now ladies and gents last but certainly not least we have Greg from Norwich." He had a small applause. "What song have you chosen Greg?" Greg whispered into Dave's ear rather than into the microphone. Dave listened to the song choice and his face froze in terror

"A..Are you sure that's your choice?" he asked, Greg nodded enthusiastically and prepared himself to sing. Dave was still standing staring at him but managed to shake himself back into reality.

"An unusual choice, ladies and gents but he's brave to go for it. Put your hands together as Greg from Norwich will be performing 'Wuthering Heights' by Kate Bush!"

Dave almost didn't want to leave the stage but he scurried off to the side to watch what was to happen. The lounge was silent as the crowd felt that something either amazing or disastrous or both was about to happen. The song started and, in an almost perfect falsetto, Greg sung every word as he floated around the stage in true Kate Bush fashion. The audience sat mesmerised by him and when he finished there was a moment of silence before the place erupted in cheers and applause. The loudest of the cheers was from Peggy and Ellie who thoroughly enjoyed the performance. No vote was needed, Dave came back on stage with the much coveted beach towel and Greg held it aloft like the world cup as he went back to his team a hero. Ellie turned round to see Kate feverishly making notes in her notebook and grinned, she had a feeling this would be making it into Kate's next book somehow.

CHAPTER 6

◆ ◆ ◆

T he next morning they awoke in the port of Toulon. Kate was standing by the window in their cabin watching the sailboats in the marina. It was a beautiful view with the town sheltered by neighbouring hills; she nursed a coffee in her hands and sighed in contentment. She had never thought of a cruise before and normally, the idea of walking tours would have her exhausted before she even started but she and Ellie had planned their excursions well. It worked out that for every day of walking there was a day of either complete rest or a seated tour so that her fatigue wouldn't take over. She loved that Ellie had considered that. She smiled as she felt two arms circling her waist and a gentle kiss placed on her neck.

"You ready to go?" murmured Ellie.

"Yes I am, let's get this show on the road. I can't wait to see the gale force hangover that my mother will be travelling with on this bright and sunny morning" she grinned evilly. Ellie laughed

"Oh yeah it's going to be fun considering they've signed up for a wine tasting tour. Let's go meet them."

They found Aggie and Peggy in the queue for the gangway. The cheerful and fresh faced excitement of Aggie brought disappointment regarding the hangover. Ellie didn't know how she did it; she would have needed an exorcist to recover her from that.

Jen was standing at the front of the queue, directing everyone to the correct tour buses, with a clipboard in hand. She pointed them to the coach for the village of Le Castellet. There was to be a village market tour followed by a tour of the local vineyard. They boarded the coach and took their seats, Peggy looked around and then grunted in annoyance.

"Hmmph look who else is on this tour, those two poisonous old bags" she directed them to the Queen and Queen mother who were sat near the back. "I don't know why they are going on trips, I mean look at them! They look as if they are heading to the execution chamber and not a lovely day out." Ellie silently agreed, she studied them for a little longer as Peggy and Aggie turned to the views of the beautiful marina. The Queen mother was glaring at the Queen and whispering to her. The Queen seemed just as angry and whispered back. This silent argument continued for a few more minutes before they spotted Ellie. They glared at her but remained silent from then on. Kate nudged Ellie.

"You ok honey?" Ellie turned back to Kate and smiled

"Yeah; I'm fine, I just don't understand what is wrong with those two. Peggy is right, why do they bother coming if they are just going to be miserable. It doesn't make sense."

"Maybe they aren't normally like this. We don't know their situation; they could have had bad news or something." Kate said reasonably "How about we don't follow their example and enjoy today. I can't wait to see the village, it has a medieval church and the cottages make it feel like time has stood still." Kate's eyes were bright with excitement and Ellie couldn't help but be carried along with her enthusiasm. She laced their fingers together and placed a gentle kiss on Kate's hand.

"I think that being anywhere with you makes time stand still" whispered Ellie with a wink, Kate burst out laughing.

"That is such a cheesy line, I hope you're ashamed of it Ellie McVey!" Kate said through her laughter as Ellie joined in.

"What? You mean you aren't swooning at my words?" Ellie teased and tried to look hurt but her eyes gave her away.

"Nope, swoon free I'm afraid, you'll just have to work a bit harder on your patter for that to happen" Kate grinned as she kissed Ellie sweetly.

The moment was interrupted by shouting at the front of the bus.

"Ah I do believe I hear the dulcet tones of the Major" said Aggie as she craned her neck over the headrest to see what was going on. Whatever the argument was, it was stopped quickly by Jen who ushered the Major onto the coach.

"My good woman, I was merely suggesting to the guide that we should rush through this dreary market visit and get to the vineyards at the earliest opportunity. I mean honestly, who cares about some crumbling old buildings and a load of hippies flogging their wares in a market." He said pompously. Ellie felt Kate bristle.

"I think you'll find that some of us have come solely to see those old buildings and the market. We aren't all chomping at the bit to down free wine like an old soak!" Kate's temper had flared and Ellie touched her arm to calm her even though she agreed with what she said and was trying really hard not to laugh.

The bus went silent for a brief moment before quiet laughter covered by coughing erupted. The Major blustered but was prevented from a retort by Jen offering him a seat further down the bus. She winked at Kate as she walked past and deposited the Major in a seat a few rows in front of the royal family. He stared out the window in a huff but remained silent.

Their tour guide was Alphonse, he was a cheery little man who bounced on the balls of his feet as he talked. He rattled through the itinerary as the bus moved off. It was to be a short drive to the village and Alphonse occasionally pointed out some views of interest on the way. He showed them the Naval port that was beside the passenger port. Several Destroyer class ships were anchored there.

"If you will look to your left you will see the 17th century defensive walls built around the old town. Toulon has always been a very important port for military defence. During the Napoleonic times your naval hero Nelson blockaded the port with a large British fleet but it's ok, we forgive you now" he giggled at his own joke.

"The port was also attacked in World war two by the German Luftwaffe and large parts of the area were bombed to destruction. The French Navy had to scuttle their fleet anchored here to make sure it wasn't captured." He continued to explain local history as Peggy turned around in her seat to talk to Kate and Ellie

"He seems awfully proud of this port considering it's really unlucky for the French. Besieged, bombed and abandoned. It's not a great advertisement is it?" she said thoughtfully

"Maybe he was routing for the British and the Germans" quipped Ellie.

They drove past the beautiful Mont Faron and watched cable cars as they ascended and descended slowly. Kate and Ellie sat quietly enjoying the view until the coach finally pulled into a carpark beside the market. They got off the coach and were instructed by Alphonse that they had some free time to wander around the market before he directed them in a tour of the medieval church. Aggie was off like a greyhound dragging Peggy along behind her as she darted towards a scarf stall. Kate and Ellie took a more leisurely pace stopping occasionally to look at some crockery or medieval style silver rings which they both took a liking to so bought one for each other.

"Oooh do I hear wedding bells?" asked Aggie excitedly from behind them. Ellie laughed

"Aggie do you honestly think that if I was going to propose to Kate that I would buy her a ring off a market stall while she is standing beside me? Come on, I would put a bit more effort into it" Ellie scoffed.

"Oh you would huh?" quipped Kate quietly, a small smile on her face.

"Uh...well.....uh....." Ellie stared wide-eyed, her brain had shut down. Kate burst out laughing and stretched to kiss Ellie on the cheek.

"Calm down Ellie, I'm not expecting a proposal.....not yet anyway." She winked and walked away to another stall leaving Ellie still in shock.

"Smooth, very smooth Detective" whispered Peggy as she pushed Ellie forwards.

They met up with Alphonse at the edge of the market and he started the tour. Alphonse takes them through the narrow streets of the village. The buildings were incredibly old and made of large stone pieces. There were several boutique shops mixed in with the houses. A cat was sunning himself in the window of a house they passed. They were shown the ancient well that provided the village with its drinking water and then they stopped at a plateau to take in the view. It was truly breath taking. Rolling green hills were spread out beneath them and vineyards were dotted in the distance. It felt as if this sleepy village had bypassed the 21st century and Kate loved every part of it.

Alphonse continued with the tour and tells them of its history and the tales of local battles as he led them to the medieval church. Peggy takes a few pictures of the church and the cottages and then some of Kate and Ellie standing in front of the church smiling happily. The Major was standing not far off from them looking bored. He turned to Alphonse

"Why isn't the F1 racing track on this tour? That would have been much more interesting than some crumbling buildings. We have those back home you know." He kept nudging Alphonse as he spoke.

"Monsieur we do not have permission to enter the track as testing is done there. Besides, there is little demand for it." Alphonse then moved away and found Jen to chat to. The Queen and Queen mother were glaring at the still loudly complaining Major who had now changed his argument and wanted to immediately go to the vineyard. The tour was over anyway so Aggie and Peggy joined the party heading up to the vineyard as Kate and Ellie walked back towards the village to grab something to eat.

The vineyard had 80 acres of vines, mainly for red and rose wines. They were directed to the owner named Marie who had set up a tasting event for the tour. They were given deep red wines and Marie started to describe the different flavours produced by each grape

"If you gently sip you will catch a hint of vanilla and the taste of oak..." she began

"Actually I think you'll find that the flavours are cherry and coffee" said the Major in his full authoritative tone.

"Sir I can assure you that..." Maria attempted to halt him but failed

"Yes, yes dear you've done very well" he said so condescendingly that Peggy wanted to strangle him for his rudeness.

"How about you leave this to an expert now, so as I was saying this red is full bodied and the flavours are cherry and.."

A big welsh man by now had had enough and stepped in. "Hey!! The lady is kind enough to try to teach us about the grapes. At least have the manners and decency to listen!" The Major huffed and blustered at the man before declaring

"I'll have you know that I am a renowned expert in red wine. I have conducted many talks on the subject at the Rotary club.." Peggy now steps in gathering her full height.

"This lady is the owner of the vineyard. This vineyard as you will know seeing as you are the expert, has been running successfully for 200 years. Her family know this land and these grapes better than anyone else on the planet so shut up and learn something. Now love, you were talking about the Merlot." She directed her question to Marie with a wink.

Marie looked like she could have kissed Peggy. She smiled in thanks and continued on with her description, The Welshman who stood easily 6ft4 glowered at the Major to ensure his silence for the rest of the tour.

Back on the bus and away from the Welsh giant's glare, the Major appeared to get some of his bluster back. Peter and Rose were chatting amiably to a couple beside them but kept looking back towards the loud voice of the Major, who was moaning at Jen.

"I mean just how ridiculously rude the customs are on the continent. I was simply trying to teach the good woman the correct flavours of the wine. She will run that vineyard into the ground you mark my words." Jen listened as long as she could tolerate. Ellie watched her, although she had a placid smile on her face, her eyes were cold. It had startled Ellie as Jen usually had a warm demeanour. She excused herself, making the excuse of a head count and went towards the front of the coach to sit with Alphonse. He stayed mercifully silent much of the remainder of the journey. That was until he saw Rose open a packet of trial mix.

"What the hell do you think you are doing you complete imbecile?!!" he bellowed at her. "No foods are to be eaten on the coach, how dare you be so selfish!!" His face was flush with anger. Thankfully the coach was arriving at the dock at that very moment. Rose put the mix back in her bag flustered and on the verge of tears. Peter looked ready to punch him into the middle of next week; but the Major had calmed the moment Rose put the snack away. They quietly all started to file out of the coach that was now parked in front of the ship.

Kate was gingerly attempting to get down the steep steps of the coach; Ellie was waiting at the bottom for her with her hand out for Kate to take. Just then, the Major barged past Kate on the steps causing her to stumble. Ellie caught her just before she reached the ground. A fury rose in her that she had never felt before in her life. She grabbed the scruff of the Major's neck and growled into his face

"You never barge past a lady, you never cause a person to fall! I don't know what regiment you were in but you are a disgrace to it- Now apologise!!" Kate had never seen Ellie so angry and touched her arm lightly to calm her. The effect was instant and she released the Major who looked terrified of Ellie. Aggie had no such qualms and soundly slapped him in the face. The Major stormed off immediately as Ellie held Kate close.

CHAPTER 7

◆ ◆ ◆

T hat evening they decided that early dinner and then a show was needed to lift the mood from the fiasco of the trip. They found a table in the buffet lounge and each went up to load a plate with food. They were half way through their meal when Peggy nudged Ellie and directed her gaze towards the door. The Major had just walked in looking red and angry. He saw them watching him and gave them a wide berth as he headed directly to the buffet. He once again, asked what was in every dish before he settled on the same British type of food that he had eaten the night before. He sat at a table and ate alone. Ellie noticed that people at several other tables were watching him; Peter and Rose plus their new friends from the coach were giving him occasional glares. The Welsh giant's jaw was flexing as he stared at him, his wife would occasionally pat his arm to bring him back to a calm state. Even the Queen and the Queen Mother were whispering and pointing out him with dark looks. They stopped abruptly when they caught Ellie looking at them. The Americans were in the corner not looking at anyone but pointing to notes on their table. Ellie looked away but noticed that Peggy was side eyeing them for a while too.

"He's certainly made himself popular on this ship hasn't he?" mused Aggie. The others nodded in agreement.

"I can understand how he could have been having an argument outside our room now, the man is a fight waiting to happen!" Kate exclaimed, still irritated at his rude behaviour. "I have a feeling that the next victim in my book is going to be an army Major" she joked.

Ellie laughed "How are you going to kill him? Please tell me its gruesome."

"I'm sure I can find something suitable for him" Kate responded with an evil smile rubbing her hands in glee.

"Ladies I think it's time we headed to the theatre before Kate's brain goes into sociopath mode" quipped Aggie as she stood and gathered her bag and shawl. The rest followed her out the door and towards the theatre. The poster outside the theatre stated that it was to be a Burlesque show this evening. Ellie turned to Kate with a mischievous grin and whispered into her ear,

"I was wondering when the saga swingers would get their entertainment in."

Kate shushed her as they went in to find a table. Considering that the show wouldn't be starting for another 20 minutes, the place was very busy already. The found a booth in the middle and sat down, Aggie ordered cocktails and lemonades for the table. Kate rested her head on Ellie's shoulder for a while, enjoying the comfort and closeness that it provided. The day had really zapped her energy. Her left leg was weak and she had felt it necessary to bring her walking stick along this evening just to give her a bit of support. She watched waiters nip in between tables delivering drinks orders and waved to Peter and Rose as they found seats right at the front. The lights dimmed and the show began. Ellie wrapped her arm around Kate and pulled her close so that she would be comfortable.

The show was much better than Kate was expecting it to be, she had envisioned some 'Carry on' style show laden with innuendo but it was a tasteful burlesque performance. The ladies were covered in the important places and the dances were subtle but striking. There was a dancer situated in a large champagne glass and Kate was amazed that she managed to keep her balance in it. The end of the show brought a standing ovation from the audience, Peter held up a rose for the closest performer on stage to accept and beamed happily when she took it gracefully.

It wasn't late when they exited the theatre and the decision was made (by Aggie) that they should have a little nightcap to end the evening. The mermaid lounge looked rowdy and full so they avoided it and headed to the other side of the ship. They found the show lounge open on deck 11 and it was a lot quieter in there. The lounge was lit by table candles and the sounds of quiet chatter were mixed with the sound of jazz being played softly on the piano in the corner.

They settled themselves at a table close to the bar and as Peggy and Aggie discussed the show at length, Kate was drinking a decaf coffee and listening to their conversation. Ellie was dipping in and out of the conversation as a louder voice from the bar kept interrupting her ability to listen to them. She turned her head slightly to locate the offending voice. She frowned as she spotted the Major talking loudly to an elderly man at the bar.

"It's a fully bodied wine this, you take it from me Nigel you won't find a nicer bottle on this ship than this one. It goes well as an evening tipple. I tried to explain the finer points to that woman at the vineyard today but you can't say anything to women these days without someone jumping down your throat. Feminists gone mad Nigel, I'm just glad I never married. They are poisonous creatures."

Nigel looked uncomfortable with this conversation and kept looking around for someone to save him, he tried to change the topic of conversation in the hopes that the Major might be more agreeable on a different subject.

"Major will you be going on the gin tour when we dock at Savona tomorrow?" The Major looked disgusted at this question, he then guffawed loudly and slapped Nigel on the back, spilling his whiskey over him.

"Good god no man! I will be doing no such thing. Horrible stuff gin, mothers ruin it was called and I firmly agree with that name. No I'm not leaving the ship tomorrow, let the riff raff enjoy that trip without me." As he said that, he had turned towards Ellie's table and looked at each of them as if they were a bad smell under his nose then turned away again. Nigel caught this and, catching Ellie's eye, mouthed an apology to her. Nigel then made his excuses and left, making sure to pass Ellie's table and quietly say to her

"Don't listen to that old windbag, he's been acting like a pompous know-it-all since he arrived here. Enjoy your evening ladies." He smiled at her and then left.

Ellie was delighted that Peggy and Aggie hadn't heard the misogynistic ramblings and that they were finally ready to turn in. They walked past the Major without a word and headed to bed.

The next morning, they woke in the port of Savona. The view from the ship was of a beautiful cove. Several of the ancient buildings in the town were large towers and there was a beautiful rambling style to the town. Kate and Ellie were heading to Genoa to take in the sights and have a leisurely exploration of the city. Aggie and Peggy were off on the gin distillery tour in Moncalieri 'to sample local delicacies'. Kate turned to both of them before they boarded the bus

"I'm warning you two right now, behave yourselves at that distillery"

This warning was met with identical 'who me?' faces from both ladies.

"Yes both of you, I still remember the last time you two 'sampled' gin. I don't need to be explaining to the local gendarme why you're both topless and singing dirty limericks. Ellie burst out laughing as Peggy and Aggie looked mortified that they could be accused of such behaviour. Kate didn't back down and finally Peggy responded

"That was a one-off! It was a bad batch of gin I'm sure of it. Don't be ridiculous Kate dear we will be perfectly well behaved" she said snootily.

"Uh huh, you better" Kate responded with her arms folded and her eyebrow raised. Peggy was about to respond but Aggie pulled her by the arm towards the coach

"Learn when you're beat Peggy dear."

Kate and Ellie waved at them through the coach window. The Queen and Queen mother boarded next followed by Peter and Rose and then Jen followed with her clipboard. She gave them a little wave as she walked up the steps of the coach. Ellie thought that Jen looked very happy today, it must be because the Major wasn't to be joining them. They turned and walked towards their own coach which would be taking them on to Genoa. As they boarded they noticed the Welsh giant and his wife, he smiled and asked them to sit across the aisle from them which Kate and Ellie did.

"Girls I would like to apologise for yesterday" he started quietly. Ellie looked baffled "Why would you need to apologise Mr...?"

"Oh Jenkins, Owain Jenkins and this is my wife Barbara" they shook hands and Kate and Ellie introduced themselves.

"Pleasure to meet you, I'm apologising because I usually don't let my temper get away from me. That man got me so angry yesterday that if you hadn't grabbed him when you did, I would have punched him there and then. Are you ok after your tumble Kate?"

"Yes I'm fine thank you, and you have no reason to apologise Owain. The Major has absolutely no manners, there's no fixing that at his age." Kate responded.

"Still, I feel like I should have said or done more. I hate bullies, always have. I was picked on at school because I was a bit over-weight and I've always tried since then to call out bullying be-haviour when I see it. I played professional rugby for a while and I hope that I kept the dressing room a friendly place" Owain was a big teddy bear, he flushed red after his speech and then laughed quietly.

"Sorry, I went off on a little tangent there. Are you two enjoying your holiday?"

"Yes, it's been lovely so far, well except for that incident yester-day. It's been better than we expected I think" responded Ellie with a smile.

The coach moved off and the Jenkins turned to watch the scen-ery. Kate laced her fingers with Ellies and rested her head on her shoulder and nodded off. She woke an hour later as the bus dropped them at the Piazza de Ferrari. They were to meet back at the coach in 3 hours to return to the ship.

They strolled through the square and admired the beautiful fountain situated in the middle and took several pictures of the architecture. They walked slowly hand in hand down the alley-ways and found a little restaurant with tables outside. This was to be a relaxing day with as little walking as possible so that Kate had a rest day. They sat at the table and watched tourists wandering around taking pictures. A Japanese man was getting shouted at by an Italian in a high visibility vest as he was try-ing to stand in the fountain. Their meals arrived during this argument and they took their time to enjoy the food. Kate had ordered a traditional pesto pasta dish as pesto had been created in the region. Whereas Ellie had stuck with her less adventurous palate and chose a pizza. Ellie had never tasted a better one, it was so fresh, she was now ruined for pizza back home. They continued to watch as the irate Italian had now telephoned the local police. They had arrived and were now chasing the tourist around the fountain like keystone cops. The tourist was still taking pictures as he ran. Sadly, they caught him eventually and he was escorted sideways into the police van. With their entertainment finished, they paid the bill and ordered ice cream cones to go.

They walked through the streets enjoying the sun and taking in the sights, they entered the Cattedrale di San Lorenzo and took pictures of its zebra-striped walls. Outside they spotted some stalls and Ellie bought a pashmina for her aunt and a new wallet for her dad and then they made their way back to the coach.

The journey back was quick and in no time they were boarding the ship once more. Aggie and Peggy's tour would not be back for another hour or two so they decided to go back to their room. Kate was exhausted and decided on a sleep for a few hours, the holiday taken a lot from her with the heat and all the walking. Ellie kissed her, grabbed her laptop and went out on deck to call Gavin without disturbing her.

"Alright boss, how's the HMS Titanic?" Gavin bellowed through the screen as the videocall connected.

"Funny. It's been great so far Gav, although I feel like I'm in a 1970s sitcom most of the time. There are some real characters on this ship, but I'll fill you in later. Never mind that though, how are our babies?"

On queue there was a loud "Aroooo" as Bruiser bounced up on Gavin's lap and gave a lopsided grin into the screen. Ellie smiled at his happy face.

"Hello wee man, are you behaving yourself?"

"Nope, he has the run of the place. The missus has the both of them spoiled; she actually gave them both steak for dinner last night. Steak Els!" he whined "what did I get? Ham salad, its criminal and I'm close to asking for a divorce on the grounds of mental cruelty."

"Poor baby" said Ellie laughing

"That's not all, they now sleep in the bed with us. She brings them up when I'm asleep. I woke up this morning with Bella wrapped round my head and Bruiser under the covers licking at my leg. Enough about my troubles though, are you and your better half doing ok?"

"Yeah we're fine, although I nearly strangled a bloke yesterday."

"You? That's not like you Els, you're usually Miss calm and collected. What happened? Did he slag off the X-Files or something?"

"No, it's just this obnoxious army git, he was causing a scene on one of the trips we were on. When he was getting off the coach he barged into Kate as she was making her way down the stairs and knocked her over."

"Oh no way! Is she ok? He didn't hurt her did her?" Gavin was getting protective. He loved Kate and treated her like a big sister.

"She's ok, her leg is a little sore but that's normal for her. I caught her before she landed on the ground so it could have bene worse."

"Now I understand why you had him by the throat, I would have done the same thing. What a dick, I would have knocked the bastard out Els. Who goes on holiday to be an arse like that?"

"It's not just that Gav, I'm getting an uneasy feeling, there's a lot of weird things happening on this ship that I can't quite put my finger on." She frowned

"Such as?" he asked while Bruiser was licking his chin

"There's an American couple for instance, they are dressed in proper camouflage gear and are always whispering over a map of the ship, it's just a bit weird. Another thing, the Major was threatened outside my cabin on the first night of the cruise. There seems to be a lot of bad blood stirring up and I don't know why. It's making me uneasy, I feel like it's going to come to a head somehow." She confessed.

"Just be careful Els, you don't want to be caught in the middle of anything that happens, this guy sounds like he could cause a riot in an empty room. This kind of tension is probably the norm for him. Try to relax and empty that brain of yours for the rest of the trip." He said reasonably "Now kindly bugger off as I need to take your little darlings for a walk before I head to work, enjoy yourself Els." He ended the call with two pups dancing round him. Ellie sighed, he was right, she needed to relax and stop overthinking everything.

Ellie was drinking a coffee and trying to quieten her mind a little by watching the sea. She knew Kate would be sleeping for a while longer, so she didn't want to go disturbing her as soon as she had finished her call so she got coffee. She was one of only a few passengers out on deck to watch the sun get lower in the sky. The waiters were clearing the tables to prepare for dinner. A couple of them started clearing the table next to Ellie and she picked up their conversation.

"Did Eddie find it yet?" asked the taller of the two as he collected glasses and cutlery.

"No and he's beside himself with worry. He knew he had it when he started his shift but when he returned to the cleaning cart it was gone."

"Oh he didn't leave it on the cart did he? He knows he's not supposed to do that! If Miss Blackman finds out she'll sack him for sure. He's going to have to report it missing."

"Oh, you know what Eddie is like. He's so forgetful, that's why he leaves it on the cart. More than once he's left it in a room and had to get security to let him back in to get it. Miss Blackman has already warned him for that. It's a shame really, you know he's saving up for his wedding next year. If they don't sack him then he'll have to pay for a replacement and those master keys are not cheap to replace." They moved further away to clear other tables as Ellie drained her coffee cup and headed back to her cabin.

Ellie was waiting on the lift to take her down to her cabin on deck 5 when she started to hear singing, bad singing. She peaked around the corner to the corridor that led to the rooms. She was met with the sight of Aggie and Peggy. They were being propped up in the middle by Jen as they bounced off the walls as they staggered towards their cabin singing 'Dancing Queen'.

Ellie rushed forwards to help Jen who was now buckling under the combined weight and grabbed Peggy by the waist and hoisted her up straight.

"Ellie!!! Howshmyfavourite niece in law?" slurred Peggy as she pulled Ellie down into a bear hug which unfortunately overbalanced and landed them both on the floor.

"Peggy what the hell?! I take it the gin tour was a roaring success?" she directed this question to Jen who was now trying to keep Aggie from trying to do the splits.

"Ooh yes, you could say that" grunted Jen as she half dragged Aggie to her door. Ellie grabbed the key off Peggy and opened the door. Jen and Ellie managed to drag the two inside and get them to their beds. Ellie brought the bin from the bathroom through and sat it between the beds as Jen put the ladies souvenirs away with a clink.

"They bought a few bottles at the gift shop" she explained.

"For god sake get those hidden somewhere until they sober up, the last thing we need is for ABBA here to take their show out into the rest of the ship" warned Ellie.

"Good point, I'll stick them up with the spare pillows" said Jen.

"Well it looks like they aren't fit for an evening meal so I better pop down to the buffet and bring them something up. Thanks Jen and I'm sorry if they were a handful"

"Oh they weren't a handful honestly, those women that arrived with the electric scooter were much worse. They were in a terrible mood. The only time they stopped complaining was during the talk on the different ingredients that make different gins. Your two were good as gold until the free samples stage of the tour." Jen laughed

"Oh god I've seen those two in action, once again I apologise" Ellie laughed as they left the room to let them sleep it off. She said goodbye to Jen and jogged up the corridor to the buffet were she plated up four plates onto a tray and went back to Aggie's room to drop off the food that they would really need later. She got a couple of slurred words in thanks and several tearful 'I love you Ellies' and then she left.

She got back to her cabin to find Kate awake and writing in her notebook. Kate looked up and saw the plates and frowned in confusion.

"I thought we were meeting mum and Peggy soon"

"Change of plan honey, your mother and your aunt have returned from the gin tour in a somewhat merry state."

"Oh god, how bad was it? Did they have clothes on?" she asked warily with her hands over her face.

"Thankfully yes, but they were doing their ABBA tribute whilst being carried home by Jen when I found them. We put them to bed with a couple of plates of food and hid the gin that they bought from the distillery." said Ellie as she set the plates down at the small table in the corner.

"Wise move, god knows how much trouble they could get into. Thank you for bringing dinner, I must admit I'm still a bit tired and sore so a night in is just what the doctor ordered" said Kate as she sat down at the table to eat.

"That's what I thought, are you going to be ok for the tour tomorrow? We don't have to go if you're not up to it you know" asked Ellie, concern in her eyes.

"I know, but I want to try. M.S. is something I have to live with yes but I want to still be able to have as normal a life as I can. I want to see things with you and experience life to the best of my abilities." Explained Kate as she took Ellie's hand.

"Ok honey, but we do things at a steady pace agreed?"

"Agreed" they sealed the deal with a kiss.

CHAPTER 8

♦ ♦ ♦

The next morning they woke up to the sounds of dock workers in Livorno. Ellie looked out of the window to watch men haul cargo off a boat docked at the other side of the port. The beautiful city of Livorno sprawled as far as you could see up to the hills. The sun was already shining and it looked like it was going to be a scorcher of a day.

Kate stirred after a while and, still half asleep, stumbled through to the bathroom. Ellie stifled a laugh, she thought of Aggie and Peggy ricocheting off the walls last night and the action seemed similar. She boiled the kettle for coffee and got clothes out for both of them for the day. They were heading to Pisa for a sightseeing tour. Aggie and Peggy were booked for another vineyard tour but somehow Ellie didn't think that they would be up for that today.

"Honey should I call and book the terrible twosome onto our tour today?" Ellie shouted to Kate. She heard Kate chuckle from the bathroom.

"Oh yes, those two will never make a wine tasting today. I can't wait for them to be cooped up on a bus for a few hours too." she was laughing when she came out of the bathroom and had an evil glint in her eye.

"Yeah well just make sure we aren't sitting in front of them, if they puke I want to be downwind of it" Ellie replied as she picked up the phone to call excursions. Within a few minutes the booking had been changed, Ellie made the coffee and then had a quick shower while Kate got dressed.

They went for a quick breakfast, not surprised that Aggie and Peggy were absent for this. They ate quickly and made their way down to the coaches. Aggie and Peggy were standing on the dock not far from the buses. They looked hellish, Aggie was pale with dark bags under her eyes and her cardigan was on inside out. Peggy's hair was still sticking up at the back and she was wearing odd socks with shorts.

"Ooh god this looks like a gale force hangover" Kate whispered in Ellie's ear. "I packed emergency sick bags, painkillers and water in my backpack just in case this happened. You take Peggy and I'll get mum and we will try to get them on the coach. They don't look like they will be able to move any further under their own steam."

Ellie spotted Jen at the wine tasting bus and she had an idea "Wait, I've got an idea before we do that. Come on" Ellie walked off with Kate right behind her towards the hungover baby boomers. Ellie grabbed Peggy by the arm and started to guide her towards Jen, Kate did the same with Aggie. When they reached Jen, Ellie winked at her conspiratorially before she spoke.

"Jen, I believe these two miscreants have something they need to say to you." Ellie glared at them both with her arms folded like an angry parent as Aggie and Peggy stared at their feet a little shamefaced.

"Go on" said Kate as she nudged her mum in the ribs.

"S..sorry Jen, we don't remember much after the tasting, we're sorry if we caused any trouble for you" Aggie said quietly.

"Ah that's ok, you weren't much trouble. The fire got put out eventually and the priest that you flashed isn't going to press charges" Jen said with a straight face. Any colour that had been in Aggie's face drained instantly and Ellie thought she might faint. Jen couldn't keep the straight face any longer and burst out laughing.

"I'm joking you two! No fire and no priest I swear. You were a bit giddy and we put you to bed, that's all, so you can relax. I see that your excursion has been changed for today?" she asked. Ellie confirmed to them that she had changed it for them thinking it was for the best. Peggy looked like she could have kissed her, what she did instead was hang over the dock wall and vomit into the sea.

"Delightful" groaned Kate as she tried to stay down wind of the smell while still trying to rub her aunt's back.

Jen checked her watch and looked a little irritated. Ellie caught her eye and Jen shook her head and explained.

"The Major is late again. He's the last person on this tour, we were supposed to leave 15 minutes ago but he's not turned up. I got the ships reception to call his room but he didn't answer. Honestly, I wish he could have at least informed us that he wasn't coming. It's especially irritating as he was so insistent about attending this vineyard. We're just going to have to go without him, we're already behind schedule."

"Look on the bright side; you won't have half as much trouble if he's not there. Not to mention how much quieter your day will be now that these two aren't going." Ellie stuck her thumb behind her indicating the two backsides that were now hanging over the wall emptying their stomachs into the Mediterranean.

"Good point" said Jen with a giggle "good luck with that"

They said goodbye and turned to find their own coach waiting for them.

Ellie was troubled as they got seated on their own coach. She didn't notice the conversation around her as she was deep in thought. She had an unshakeable feeling that something very wrong was happening and that the Major was at the centre of it. Her attention was caught by laughter further down the coach, Derek and Rose were regaling a couple with some hilarious tale that required a lot of demonstration and mime. Ellie watched for a while and dearly hoped that the mime being acted out by Derek was that of a sink plunger; anything other than that she didn't want to know.

They arrived at Pisa quicker than Ellie thought. She looked round to find Kate had spent the time jotting in her notebook. Ellie touched her hand gently and Kate smiled warmly at her "Ah you're back with us I see, I thought you needed thinking time so I've left you to your thoughts for a while. Are you ok sweetheart?"

"I'm fine, I just have a few niggles in my mind that won't go away."

"Do you want to share?" Kate asked as she stowed her notebook away.

"Maybe later but for now we have some exploring to do and I really want to find out who will throw up from the top of the tower first, Aggie or Peggy" she laughed as they got up and headed off the coach.

The first stop on the walking tour was the Cathedral of Santa Mary Assunta. Their guide was Giuseppe who waved a little red flag to keep everyone together through the crowds. The Cathedral was beautiful and they could see the famous leaning tower behind it. The building was truly ornate with beautiful stone and marble arches and bronze doors. Upon entry they were met with breath-taking decoration. In the basilica the ceiling had the most beautiful fresco of the Assumption of Mary. Kate had never seen a place so beautifully structured and was genuinely in awe.

Giuseppe then guided them towards the famous tower, as they walked he told them of Galileo experimenting with gravity by throwing two different sized balls from the top to prove size had no effect on how they fall. He then went on to explain that soon after construction began in the 12th century it was noticed that the tower had started to lean. When asked by a woman at the front if it would ever tip over he laughed and said no and that measures had been put in place to ensure that it never collapsed.

"Somewhere in the universe Mother Nature just said 'challenge accepted'" muttered Peggy.

The group then started to ascend the 296 steps to the top of the tower. Ellie had Kate's hand so that she could lean on her if she started to fatigue and Kate was grateful for this by the time she reached the top. Kate soaked in the tilted view of Pisa. Peggy and Aggie found the tilt too much and, looking very pale, quickly made their way back down the tower almost as soon as they had arrived. Ellie wrapped her arms around Kate and rested her chin on Kates shoulder. They stood in silence for quite a while savouring the closeness of the moment. Kate leaned back into Ellie loving the warmth and safety she found in her embrace.

"I love you" she whispered quietly.

"I love you too" was Ellie's murmured response as she kissed behind Kate's ear which earned a soft giggle. Kate was ticklish there.

They slowly made their way back down the steps hand in hand and found the hungover sisters sat on a bench in the square attempting to get their colour back. Giuseppe called them all over to say that they had a choice of free time to explore or to follow him to see the Campo Santo and the national museum. Aggie and Peggy didn't look like they would manage much more without food so they decided they would explore and find a nice café to stop for lunch. They couldn't go before Peggy got the typical funny picture of her holding up the tower. She walked away looking at the picture and chuckling at her own wit.

They found a suitable café with an outside area and ordered lunch. Peggy and Ellie decided that burgers and chips were required whereas Kate and Aggie settled for a small pasta dish each.

"We never got to ask you how the tour was yesterday, what with you both being ever so slightly tipsy when you got back" said Kate teasingly.

"Oh it was lovely!" exclaimed Aggie. "I never thought a gin tour could be so educational. It's a family owned distillery and it was so beautiful in the surrounding area. Do you know that gin was first made back in medieval times by monks to be used as a medicinal drink? They combined juniper berries and other spices. The company's most popular gin uses the lemons grown all over the Amalfi coast. They even do a gin that's blended with almonds in their wee gift shop."

"Uh huh and I presume that's what you brought back?" asked Ellie in between huge bites of her burger. She hadn't realised how hungry she was.

"Oh aye, I forgot we brought bottles back..." Peggy stopped and looked accusingly at Ellie. "Where did you put them? I don't remember seeing the bags this morning."

"Very observant of you" Ellie quipped and then laughed at the double evil glare she was getting off the older ladies. She held her hands up in surrender. "Ok they are in the cupboard behind the spare pillows. We just didn't want you both to go on a bender last night and not even get to enjoy the gin."

"How very thoughtful of you" said Aggie with a chuckle.

The rest of their time was spent wandering the narrow streets and then they met back up with Giuseppe at the coach. Ellie was taking a picture of an old man painting the view ahead of him when she felt an elbow to her ribs. She turned her head towards Kate who was not hiding her shock at what she was seeing. Ellie tracked her eye-line and it rested on Derek and Rose who were sat on a bench canoodling with the couple they had been chatting to on the journey.

"Christ she really has got us on a swingers cruise" whispered Ellie to a still dumbfounded Kate.

They arrived back at the ship at 4pm and the ship was due to sail at 5pm. The wine tour was already on board as they spotted Jen bustling down the corridor towards the stairs leading to the staff quarters. Kate and Ellie agreed to meet Aggie and Peggy at 7.30pm for dinner and then headed to their cabin.

Kate headed straight to bed once they got there for a nap and Ellie decided she would start the book she had brought with her which was a history of Pompeii. They were to be touring that region soon and she wanted to learn a bit more about the history before they arrived.

The ship had been sailing for just over an hour when Ellie heard urgent voices outside the cabin door. She looked over to Kate still sleeping soundly and got up to find out what was going on. When she opened the door she found the steward standing with the captain and another man at the Major's door. They were now talking in much softer tones about sealing the room. Ellie walked up behind them completely unnoticed and peered over their shoulders into the room. The Major was lying in the middle of the floor of his cabin motionless.

The Captain spotted her now and tried to block her view.

"Ah nothing to worry about Miss; this gentleman is feeling unwell but rest assured we are attending to him so please if you wouldn't mind returning to you cabin." He was very calm as he spoke but Ellie could read the stress on his face.

"Captain I am a Detective Chief Inspector with Police Scotland. I head up the serious crimes division so I know a dead body when I see one. What happened? I can offer you any help you need."

The Captain considered this for a moment and then seemed to give in. "Yes the man is dead I'm afraid. The steward was going in to sort out the evening turn down service and discovered him like this 10 minutes ago. This is Doctor McDonald our ships Doctor. He pronounced him dead a few moments before you arrived."

Ellie took this in and tried to scan the room quickly. The Major was in his pyjamas which she thought was strange.

"May I take a look at the body?" she enquired.

"I don't think that is necessary Miss. As far as I can tell from my cursory examination he appears to have died of natural causes." The doctor spoke in such a condescending manner that Ellie's hackles were up.

"What manner of examination could you have managed in the 5 minutes that you have been here Doctor? I don't think it's wise to make assumptions before any facts are known" Ellie responded coolly. She looked at him properly for the first time. His face was ruddy and his shirt had more than one wine stain on it. She could smell the alcohol on his breath. There was no way he was in a fit state to give a factual medical opinion.

"Captain I'm going to escort the body down to the morgue

now, it can remain there until we dock and transport can be arranged." With that he closed the cabin door and marched off with the steward in tow.

"I'm sorry Detective..."

"McVey, Ellie McVey"

"Detective McVey, I'm sorry but in these matters the Doctor has the final say on board. Unless there is proof of foul play, I can't go against his decision" said the Captain apologetically. He offered a small smile and then walked off in the same direction as the Doctor.

CHAPTER 9

◆ ◆ ◆

Kate was awake when Ellie returned to the cabin. She was putting on tan coloured tailored trousers and a white linen blouse. The natural tones brought out the beauty of her hair and the noticeable tan on her face and arms. Kate looked rested and pain free much to Ellie's delight.

"Hi honey, mum called to say they would like to have dinner a little earlier if that's ok? She appears to have found her appetite and could eat horse and saddle. That was a direct quote by the way. Where were you when I woke? I thought I could hear your voice outside."

"Somethings happened honey, the Major is dead. The Captain and the Doctor were outside. I tried to help but the Doc wasn't having it. He was drunk and arrogant but his word goes apparently. I'll get ready and we can go in a few minutes." She gave Kate a quick peck on the lips and started pulling clothes out.

"What do you mean you offered to help? Did he not have a heart attack or something?" asked Kate as she sat on the bed watching Ellie hoping on one foot trying to pull on her jeans. "You know that would go a lot quicker if you sat down to pull your trousers on."

"I've been dressing myself quite successfully for nearly 40 years my darling I think I can manage......shit!" Ellie had tripped over her trainers in the middle of the floor and stumbled over the top of the chair and disappeared behind it, legs still in the air. Kate roared with laughter as a very bemused Ellie emerged, red faced, from behind the arm chair.

"Not funny Kate, that was properly sore" she pouted as Kate laughed even harder, clutching her side "Oh god stop I've got a stitch. How have you stayed alive in your job all these years? You are the most accident prone woman I've ever met." She said through her laughter.

"Am not" came the witty retort as Ellie sat down to get her jeans on and then her shoes. She got up and dragged a still giggling Kate off the bed and out the door. The laughter returned in full force when she managed to stub her foot on the door on her way out.

At dinner Ellie told them all the details of the Major being found. When she finished she looked at Peggy who was looking thoughtfully at her.

"You don't think this was natural causes do you Ellie?" she asked shrewdly

"I honestly don't know. I admit that events leading up to this have been troubling me. A lot of people had issues with the Major, us included. I'm worried that someone might have hated him enough to kill him."

"Did you see any obvious signs of a violent death?"

"No, I didn't see any blood or obvious bruising but I only caught a glimpse of the body before the Doc stuck his oar in." she admitted.

"Well there's only one thing to do then isn't there, in order to put your mind at rest we need to see the body for ourselves."

Peggy said with a glint in her eye.

"You mean sneak down to the morgue? I don't know Peggy that's risky. I'm not sure my authority would be recognised at sea if we get caught."

"We won't get caught Ellie, have a little faith. Besides, that Doctor is no more going to stay in the morgue than I'm about to take up jogging. He will already be propping up the bar somewhere. This might be your only chance to have a proper look. Come on young'un, where's your spirit of adventure?"

"I lost it when I went head first over the chair putting jeans on earlier. You are right though, I don't think I'll get a better chance than tonight. What's the plan Peggy?"

"Well we need to figure out where the morgue is. It will obviously be below decks and out of the way. I suggest we sneak down the stairs to the crew quarters and look around" suggested Peggy.

"Or we can go straight to deck 3, room 19" said Kate from behind her phone. When everyone looked at her she rolled her eyes and turned the screen around. "Deck plans for the ship. I googled them, the morgue is beside the doctors private office on deck 3." Ellie kissed her soundly and smiled "You're a genius, this is why I love you."

"Enough of the mushy stuff please, we have things to do. Come on Ellie let's get started. Aggie would you and Kate like to meet us later in the lounge?"

"Like hell I will! I'm coming with you" responded Kate indignantly.

"Me too" agreed Aggie, her mouth set stubbornly.

"Kate this could be risky, if we are caught it could be bad for you publicity wise. Your new book is doing so well, I don't want to jeopardise that for you." said Ellie sincerely.

"I don't care about that, you're forgetting one important thing both of you. I know more about pathology than the two of you combined. The amount of research I've had to put in and all the time shadowing pathologists, I would be able to help. Please let me do this." She was determined and Ellie was torn. She wanted to protect her but she also knew Kate was right, her knowledge would be invaluable.

"Ok honey, you come with us and Aggie, we need you as lookout. Once we're in you need to be our eyes outside. Are we all ready for this?" Three overly eager faces smiled back at her and she sighed. "I was afraid of that. Come on let's go."

Most of the passengers were already in the bars or lounges enjoying the entertainment. The 'Team' as Aggie insisted on calling them, mulled around the staircase leading down to the lower decks until the coast was clear. Once the corridor was empty they quickly ran down the stairs until they reached deck 3. Ellie glanced round the corner to check the corridor was clear. Jen was walking down the corridor with another woman, Ellie was about to tell everyone to scarper but Jen and her friend turned down another corridor and disappeared. Ellie waved her team on and they crept along the corridor towards room 19. Once they got there, Ellie tried the door and it was unlocked. She posted Aggie outside and told her to knock the door if anyone was coming.

Inside the morgue was dark and cold. It was a small room with no windows. The lights flickered on automatically when they entered the room and they were met with a table and a sheet covered body. As there did not appear to be any other occupants in residence they assumed it to be the Major. Ellie walked up and carefully removed the sheet and started looking closely for any signs of struggle. She could see no blood or puncture marks, no scratches or defensive wounds. She was looking at his hands when Kate whispered to her

"I need to see his tongue; can you open his mouth for me?" Ellie did as instructed and opened the Major's mouth carefully. Rigor appeared to have been and gone as it was much easier than she thought to manoeuvre him. Kate got the torch app working on her phone and looked into his mouth.

"His tongue is very swollen, so are his lips and cheeks do you see?" she pointed these out to Peggy and Ellie "and look, he has hives around his neck too. I think he's had an allergic reaction to something and that's possibly what killed him."

"Like a bee sting or something?" Ellie asked.

"Probably not a bee sting but possibly could be an intense food allergy. It would have been very fast acting though. An allergy this severe, he would know about it and probably was very careful. No doubt he had epi pens with him, whatever he has ingested is probably still in his cabin. He would have had no more than a couple of minutes."

"Are you sure?" asked Ellie seriously.

"As sure as I can be, I'm not a doctor but I have done research on severe allergies for a book and these are classic signs."

"We need to get into his room to find out if he had epi pens or an allergy warning somewhere and also what he could have eaten or drank that caused this. I don't know how to get in though, we would need a key."

"Don't worry girls, I have a little device in my suitcase that will get us in without any difficulty" said Peggy confidently. 'Oh god' thought Ellie 'she's got that manic glint in her eyes again. That woman is truly frightening.'

Ellie, Kate and Aggie were waiting in their room while Peggy ran off to fetch her equipment from her cabin. Ellie reached over and pulled Kate closer to her and kissed her forehead softly.

"Thank you for doing this, I would never have thought of allergies. I'm glad you were with me and I'm sorry I tried to keep you out of it. I keep thinking you need protecting but I know you don't and I'm sorry for assuming that."

"Well said" offered Aggie from the couch "Oh, you have different nudey paintings in your room. Ours are mostly women bent over and getting..."

Peggy knocked on the door and Ellie has never been more thankful to finish a conversation. She let Peggy in and they kept the door open slightly to wait for the corridor to be empty. They only needed to wait a few minutes before they ventured back out into the corridor. Once again Aggie was on sentry duty. Peggy put a key card into the slot. It was attached to a tablet computer and Peggy was typing furiously away as numbers flashed up. In seconds the lock clicked and the light went from red to green. Peggy was triumphant as she opened the door and they all piled in.

Ellie flicked the lights on and looked around, nothing seemed to be out of place.

"All right gang, split up and look for clues" said Peggy excitedly.

"Gang? Clues? Peggy this isn't Scooby doo! Just have a look around and see if anything looks iffy." whispered Ellie.

"OK....why are you whispering?" asked Peggy.

"I just...you know what..j.. just shut up and look" said Ellie flustered.

Peggy started going through the drawers as Kate tried the bathroom. Ellie looked around the room, there was a jug of water on the dresser with a half full glass beside it. There was a diary beside it, Ellie picked it up and scanned the entries. The entries stopped before the cruise which Ellie thought was odd, why bring a diary and not write in it? She went back through the earlier entries, he wrote daily entries without fail. She went back to the last entry and looked closely; there was a tiny jagged edge of paper at the bottom. Pages had been torn out of the diary.

"I've found something" came the call from the bathroom. Kate emerged holding an epi pen, she was holding it with a tissue so as not to get her prints on it.

"Well that confirms that the Major did have an allergy of some kind, well done honey" Ellie said proudly as Kate blushed but gave her a pleased smile. Ellie thought back to the times she saw the Major in the buffet queue, his constant enquiries into the food made more sense now. She scanned the room again, checked the bin and down the side of the bed but she couldn't find any food anywhere. He had to have ingested something in here because it would have been an immediate reaction. Her eyes rested again on the glass of water. She walked over to it and sniffed the contents.

"Peggy can you come over and give this a smell and tell me what you think it is?" she asked. Peggy came over and took a sniff, careful not to touch the glass. She looked up in surprise "It's gin."

Before they could say anything else frantic knocking came from the door. Their sentry was warning them but it was too late, they heard Aggie trying to divert him but the steward opened the door catching them in the act.

CHAPTER 10

◆ ◆ ◆

The Captain was pacing up and down his office in front of the women. He looked like a disappointed headmaster, Ellie thought it best to try to explain their actions before he wore a hole in his carpet.

"Captain I know it was unorthodox to do what we did but I needed to know. Quite frankly I didn't trust the judgement of an intoxicated ships Doctor in this matter. We have been able to determine that we believe the Major died from an allergic reaction to something he ate or drank. In his room we found epi pens to confirm allergies. We found a glass of gin which is totally out of character as he was heard saying that he couldn't stand the stuff and would never drink it. His most recent diary entries have been removed and they are not in his room. To be frank, I am concerned about this death and I would like your permission to investigate it a little further."

The Captain listened to all of this and finally stopped pacing. He sat in his char facing Ellie.

"Detective I admit this is concerning, although I still believe this to be an unfortunate accident. You have my permission to investigate, I would rather you did that and found nothing than me doing nothing where there could potentially be an issue. As we are at sea you have jurisdiction in this matter as we are a British registered vessel. If you need anything, please come to me and I would like to be informed of any findings. Does that seem fair?"

"It does, thank you Captain. I will try to be discreet in my investigations until I can be certain as to the manner of death."

It was late when they finally left the Captain's office, they had all planned to go ashore in Corsica the next day but Ellie thought it best if she stay on board and look into a few things but she makes sure the rest of them go and enjoy the day. As Ellie was falling asleep that night the gin glass whirled in her mind.

Ellie awoke with several questions formed in her mind; what was the Major allergic to? Who would have known this information? Was this accidental? Why was there gin in his room when he detested it? Who had access to his room? She was determined to find answers. She went to breakfast with Kate before she left to explore Corsica.

"Honey are you sure you don't want me to stay here? I don't mind and maybe I could help." asked Kate as she stirred her coffee.

"You've already helped me and I will need your help again but not until I get more facts, there's no point in both of us missing out of some sun and relaxation. Hopefully if I get some information then I can still meet you in a few hours. My main aim is to figure out his allergy, once I know that then I can figure out how he managed to ingest whatever it is." Kate was thoughtful for a few moments and then her face brightened up.

"I've got it! Do you remember on the flight out that we were told that a passenger had a severe nut allergy? The Major was on our flight, he always stuck with traditional meals like beef and potatoes didn't he? Think of the other options we've had, chicken satay and kormas and things like that. All things with peanuts or almonds in them."

"You are an absolute genius, if you ever want to give up writing you would make an excellent private investigator" said Ellie as she kissed Kate gently. "I think you've nailed it, I just need to figure out where he would have come into contact with nuts."

Aggie and Peggy arrived as Ellie was deep in thought, she felt like the answer was swimming in front of her but she couldn't quite connect the dots. Kate was filling the others in on what they had figured out so far. When she heard Kate talking about peanuts and almonds again it suddenly clicked.

"The gin!" she said excitedly and loud enough to make Aggie jump and clutch her chest.

"Bloody hell Ellie I wish you would warn me when you're going to do that, you've just taken five years off my life with a start like that!" Aggie grumbled as she massaged her chest melodramatically. Ellie muttered an apology and asked them to stay there and not leave without her. She bolted from the table and ran along to the lifts and punched the buttons impatiently. In the end she gave up and tore down the stairs and along to the Captains office. She knocked and entered as the Captain got up from his seat to greet her but she cut him off in her haste.

"Sorry Captain, I think I've figured out what the Major had to cause his reaction and if I'm right, I think he may have been deliberately poisoned." She exclaimed. The Captain took a moment to process this and then asked

"What do you need me to do Detective?"

"I need to take a small sample of the water jug contents from his room. I need to give it to our resident expert for a taste confirmation"

"Taste confirmation? Would that not be dangerous if indeed the man met with foul play?"

"No I assure you that the contents on that jug were only harmful to the Major. Do I have your permission?"

"Of course, here I've got a pass key for you. It will get you into his cabin. Please let me know what your findings are. If you think this is foul play then I need to notify the authorities back in the UK and at Palma."

She thanked him and left to go to the Majors cabin, thankfully the Captain had ordered the room to be left untouched so the jug was still sitting on the dressing table. She poured a small amount into a coffee cup and then returned to the dining room where her family were still sitting where she left them.

"I needed an expert for this" she explained as she sat down. She handed the cup to Aggie. "Aggie I need to know what flavours you get from this when you taste it. You are an amazing cook and I know you taste individual flavours in drinks, I need your expertise"

Aggie looked doubtful but she put the cup to her lips and tasted a small amount of the liquid.

"It's gin, although it has an unusual flavour. I can taste the juniper and the lemon but there's something else." She took another sip and finally hit on the elusive ingredient. "It's almond gin. I remember that taste when we were on the tour. It has a slightly sweeter taste than the usual gin. Yes its unmistakable Ellie, it's the almond gin from the distillery"

Ellie sat back with a grim expression. "It's murder then. There is no way the Major would touch gin let alone risk almond gin. He was far too cautious for that kind of mistake. Someone has given it to him, someone who either was on that tour or heard about it and wanted the Major gone.

CHAPTER 11

◆ ◆ ◆

E llie waved the others off on their day exploring and she promised she would catch up with them soon. She went back to her cabin and loaded up her laptop and called Gavin.

"Hey there boss, two calls in a week, are you missing me?" he said as he batted his eyelashes as her. The effect was somewhat diminished as he had brown sauce on his chin.

"Oh yeah, how could I not miss such manliness and beauty." She deadpanned. "You've got sauce on your chin mate" He wiped it with his finger and tried to seductively lick it off. Ellie burst out laughing.

"You are so gross. Concentrate, I've got something I need you to find out for me"

"Sure, what do you need boss lady?" he got a pen ready to take notes.

"I need you to find out all you can on a Major Edward Charleston."

"Sure, what's he done? Did he cheat at bridge or something?" he joked

"Nope he died."

"How inconsiderate of him. Why are you involved?"

"He died from an allergic reaction that I think was an intentional act to cause him harm. I need more information on the man in order to investigate fully. He wasn't a pleasant man to deal with, hell I almost choked the life out of him. I know there are several people on board that disliked him. I just need to find out if any of them had motive to kill him."

"No problem Els, we're kind of quiet at the moment anyway so I'll get this to you as quickly as I can."

"Thanks for that, how are my babies today?"

"Currently getting spoiled at posh pups spa. The missus has taken them off for pampering and a groom, Bruiser decided to roll in something funky at the park so it was probably for the best. I'll send you pictures when I get home."

"Sounds good, I better head now. I promised that I would meet the others in the market as soon as I was done. Do you want anything brought back?"

"Anything sweet, you know me" he grinned.

They hung up and Ellie got herself ready for a more relaxing part of her day.

Ellie stepped off the ship into the warm sunshine of Ajaccio. She walked along to the yacht moorings at the end of the dock where the wealthy paid a fortune to moor. The local market was across the road from the docks and she soon caught up to the others as they were browsing a stall that sold nougat.

"Madame please, you 'ave tried every flavour of nougat we 'ave 'ere" the vendor pleaded with a French accent.

"Yes yes young man, no need to rush me. This is an important decision, if I'm to show people back home how wonderful your product is then I need to make sure I pick the best one. I'm trying to advertise on your behalf in Scotland so I really don't see why you are so impatient...Oh really now, why are you crying?" asked Peggy astonished as the young vendor started bawling at the top of his lungs in frustration.

"Looks like I've arrived just in time" said Ellie from behind them. "She will buy one of each flavour." She glared at Peggy who looked ready to argue but wisely held her tongue and started counting out euros. The vendor happily handed over a large bag full of nougat to Peggy who grumbled and moved off to the next stall. The vendor motioned for Ellie and when she got to him he handed her a large bag of candied almonds and then hugged her.

"Merci madame et bon chance!" he waved her off.

Kate was standing close by with a smile on her face, she looped her arm into Ellie's and steered her in the direction that Peggy had headed.

"Thank you for that, Peggy was winding him up, the poor man. That woman will do anything for a freebie. This is why she isn't allowed at Costco anymore, she got barred for harassing the chocolate pretzel woman."

Ellie laughed, she was picturing Peggy running at full pelt after some poor woman with a tray of pretzels. They caught up with Aggie and Peggy at a honey stall. Aggie was selecting some honey to use in baking as was experimenting with sugar free cakes.

"So did you get any information after we left?" Kate asked as they continued to walk slowly around the market.

"Not yet, I called Gavin and asked him to dig up some information on the Major. I'm thinking if we know more about his background then we could maybe understand why someone wanted to harm him."

"That makes sense; although would you class this as a premeditated crime? I mean who would have known he was going to be on the cruise? If they knew him well enough to know his holiday plans, would it not be easier to harm him anywhere else and at any other time than when the number of possible suspects is cut due to the fact that no outsider could have got on board to do this."

"I agree that whoever did this had no idea he was to be on this cruise. I think they just happened to be here. I think this was going to be their only chance at getting close to him so they had to act quickly. The purchasing of the gin is enough premeditation for me. I need to start narrowing the suspect list down, I'll make a start when we get back to the ship later.

Aggie and Peggy caught up with them as they walked down the street adjacent to the sea, they stopped at a large marble statue. It was a man holding up a shield in a protective pose. There was a dedication in the plinth in French that Ellie could understand some of but not the full statement. She was about to google it when Peggy spoke softly

"To those who gave their lives for a free race and France"

"The French resistance?" asked Ellie

"Yes, they were prolific in Corsica at the time. Did you know that not one Jewish person was killed during the war on Corsica? They were always protected by the Corsican people" explained Peggy still looking at the statue.

"Amazing bravery" said Kate and Ellie nodded in agreement. She took pictures of the monument taking care to include the dedication.

"Wait a minute, you speak French?" asked Kate to her aunt

"Yes dear I do, but technically that translation is Corsican not French" explained Peggy as she walked off towards a supermarket leaving the others standing.

Once they had picked up chocolate provisions for their cabins they were all back on board the ship hunting down a good spot to spend the afternoon in the sun. They found some sunbeds on deck close to the lido bar and settled in. Kate and Aggie started a game of gin rummy while Peggy watched the yachts sailing out at sea. Ellie got out her notepad and started noting down names of anyone she could think of that had any negative interactions with the Major. She noted that the Welsh couple had a run in with him and the Queen and Queen mother seemed more angry than usual in his presence. Peter and Rose had issues with him, as had Ellie (she put her own name up too) and finally Jen who seemed vexed by his actions and she had just started with the ship on this cruise.

As Ellie was thinking she looked up and spotted the American couple, they were in jeans today for a change but were attempting to open a staff only door. They didn't seem to have any luck and the male kicked it in frustration before they stormed off gesticulating angrily. Ellie quickly added them to her list, not because of any argument with the Major but purely for the fact that she was uneasy about their actions.

She decided that the best way to narrow this down would be to find out who had the opportunity to kill the Major. Alibis would be hard to get in an unofficial capacity, she would need to steer the conversation somehow. She spotted Jen taking an aqua aerobics class by the pool and decided to make her move. Jen would have the easiest means of accessing the Major's cabin as she was staff. Ellie waited until the class was over and followed Jen over to the bar.

"Hi Jen, don't you ever get a day off from this place?" Ellie asked light-heartedly. Jen laughed as she grabbed a bottle of water.

"Aye, I get some time off occasionally."

"I should hope so, you work so hard. Do you ever get to go off-shore without taking all of us on a tour?"

"To be honest I like the tours, I get to see so many cool things that I would probably miss if I was just bumbling about on my own."

"Good point, how did the gin tour go by the way? Apart from my in-laws being pests"

"It was very interesting actually, I was surprised. Your in laws weren't pests, just….enjoying everything there was to offer" she said tactfully.

"Uh huh. Thankfully they didn't manage to drink the gifts they brought back. Did you buy any?"

"Oh yes, well most of us did. It was delicious gin and very reasonably priced. I don't think anyone left without buying a bottle or two."

'Damn' thought Ellie, she decided to change the conversation.

"Isn't it awful about the Major, being found dead in his cabin." She asked innocently.

"Oh yes it's terrible for him, such a shame to die alone I always think."

"Yes, terrible. Did you know him well?"

"No not at all, I only met him on the tours."

"He didn't seem to ingratiate himself to many people, I noticed that you weren't too fond of the old boy either?" Ellie asked

"No…if I'm honest I didn't like him. He got a bit…you

know....handsy on the coach and I had to shut that down quickly. He wasn't pleasant, I'm sad for his death but I can't say I'll miss him."

"I don't blame you at all. After a long tour like that did you at least get the night off or did you have to work some more?"

"No I was working, as soon as the tour was back and I had delivered your in-laws home I had to help out at the excursion desk taking bookings for the next day. I was there until 8 o'clock I think, and then I had dinner and went to bed. I had to get up early to set up for the tours again."

"Well I hope your roommate was quiet enough to let you rest."

"Oh she's on the same shift pattern as I am; it makes it easier for us to manage the living arrangements. We were both in the room early and asleep. I better go Ellie, I'm due to judge the groovy grandad competition soon."

"Tell me you're joking" asked Ellie astonished, Jen laughed "I wish I was."

CHAPTER 12

◆ ◆ ◆

Ellie was making her way back to her sunbed when she was met by Kate.

"Aunt Peggy has found out there's a quiz starting at the poolside so she's making us move" she explained. At the pool Ellie spotted Derek and Rose sitting at a table ready for the quiz. She quickly made a move in their direction and nabbed the table beside them, ensuring she sat at the seat closest to them. When Kate caught up with her she was about to ask why she took off so quickly but Ellie winked at her and nodded in Derek's direction. Kate understood and took the seat beside her. Peggy and Aggie came bustling along soon after. Aggie managed to find a waiter for the drinks order and then sat down and took out her knitting. Peggy was already in the zone for the quiz.

"Ladies and gentlemen welcome to the pool side quiz. Today we are going to be playing charades! The clues will be acted out by your very own entertainment crew. All you have to do is write down what you think they are acting. Can you give a warm round of applause for your entertainment crew Steve, Millie and Janice! We will begin in a few moments; we just need to sort them out with some props."

While they were waiting Ellie started chatting to Rose.

"Hello you two, enjoying your holiday so far?" she asked cheerily.

"Oh yes it's been smashing! We've met such lovely people on board, in fact we've already booked up to come again next year with a couple we've met" said Rose happily. 'I bet you have' thought Ellie as she supressed a smile.

"I'm glad you've met some nice people, there are some rather unpleasant characters about and I..." Ellie was interrupted by Rose pointing at the scene being acted out for the quiz. Steve was running around with a fin on his back chasing after a screaming Millie.

"Oh Derek we know this one! It's Debbie does Dallas!"

"Yes of course, well done Rose I'll write it down" Derek exclaimed happily. Ellie looked between the two of them bemused for a second and then shook her head to clear it. "I'm sorry Ellie what were you saying?" said Rose

"I was just about to ask if you had heard the awful news about the Major?" Ellie decided subtlety would not work on this pair.

"Yes, it is dreadful isn't it? Dying on your holiday, dying should be kept for wet Tuesdays in January not on a lovely cruise" said Rose sadly.

"Indeed, I mean he wasn't a nice man and we all had run-ins with him but still it's sad. Did you happen to go on the gin tour? We missed it and those two were in a delicate state when they arrived home so we didn't get many details about it" Ellie joked.

"Yes we went on the gin tour, if we're honest, the only reason we went is because we knew the Major wouldn't be there. Is that a bad thing to say about someone recently deceased? Oh well, no point in lying I suppose, we weren't planning on going on any trip that he was doing. After him shouting at me, I didn't fancy spending any more time in his company. And then he called us perverts just because we enjoy a bit of company now and then! The gin tour was perfect; we enjoy a tipple when we're entertaining guests if you know what I mean. That gift shop had a lovely selection so we brought a few bottles back for one of our next parties."

"I'm glad you had fun, and I'm sorry that the Major called you that. No doubt he would probably have said the same about us" Ellie joked. "Did you get to see the show that night at the theatre?"

"No we were um....entertaining some friends in our room that evening. In fact it became an all-nighter didn't it Derek?"

"Indeed it did, we were exhausted the next day. We are getting a little bit too old for all night parties I'm afraid Ellie" he smiled.

"I'm glad you had fun, what do you call this couple you were with? Just so that I can say hello in passing" Ellie asked innocently.

"It's Mr and Mrs Burrows, lovely broad minded couple from the Cotswolds"

"I'll look out for them to say hello, I best get back to this quiz. I can feel Peggy's eyes burning a hole in the back of my head" she turned back to her own table and noted down the Burrows' name as a potential alibi to track down.

Without her help, Peggy had been doing the quiz alone. Kate was writing and Aggie wasn't interested so Peggy was in a little huff for the rest of the afternoon.

After the quiz finished the rest of the group went back to their cabins. Ellie was strolling along all the public decks trying to 'accidentally' bump into either the Welsh couple or their Majesties but she had no luck. They must still be off the ship.

Ellie was heading back to her cabin to meet up with Kate who had gone on to take a shower when the Captain caught up with her in the corridor.

"Ah Detective, how is your investigation going?"

"Please Captain, call me Ellie, if anyone hears you call me Detective they won't speak to me in the same way" she pleaded.

"Oh I'm sorry, Ellie how are you getting on?" he corrected himself.

"Well I've requested some information on the Major from my partner back in Scotland and I've got some alibis to check up on. You could help with that actually. Could you give me the staff rota for Jen and her roommate, the new member of your crew that does the tours?"

"Jen?....ah yes Jen she's an asset to the crew...surely you don't think..." he looked horrified.

"Captain I don't think anything right now, I'm just narrowing down possibilities and sadly that includes the crew. I would also like to talk to the steward in charge of the Major's room when convenient."

"Certainly, Eddie is on shift at the moment but I'll get a message to him to come and see you. I've also took the liberty of setting up an office for you in the library. I've closed it off so that you will be undisturbed."

"Thank you Captain, I appreciate all your help." She said goodbye and went into the cabin to get ready for dinner.

"Did you find anyone else to speak to?" asked Kate from the bathroom as Ellie slumped on the bed.

No, I'm sure I've walked miles around this bloody barge and no sign of anyone I needed to see." Ellie moaned. "But the Captain is going to give me the rota and let me speak to the steward. He's got me a little office set up too."

"Very fancy, hopefully you will have better luck at dinner.

They've all got to be back on board by then so it should be easier." said Kate consolingly. She had emerged from the bathroom in jeans and a sparkly top, her hair was straightened and framed her face beautifully. Ellie reached up and pulled her into a hug, her face nuzzled at Kate's stomach and she breathed deeply. The smell of apple from her soap instantly relaxed Ellie. She didn't want to go out to eat, she just wanted to stay here with Kate alone and comfortable. Sadly her stomach had other ideas and grumbled loudly making Kate giggle.

"We better feed that monster, come on"

The dining room was full but they managed to grab a table near the door. Ellie was looking around but still couldn't find the people she needed to talk to. She got up and joined the queue for the Indian cuisine and, by luck, was standing behind Mr and Mrs Burrows. 'Thank God something has went right tonight!' she thought. She waited until they were getting plates before she made her move.

"Mr and Mrs Burrows?"

"Yes that's us." Mr Burrows was a tall man with a protruding Adams apple; his wife was no more than 5ft 1. They looked like teachers so it was all the more amusing that they appeared to be swinging friends!

"I'm sorry we've not been introduced, I'm Ellie. I'm a friend of Derek and Rose, they said I should say hello if I ever spot you so that's exactly what I've done." Ellie said in a cheery manner.

"Well that's a nice thing to do, hello to you Ellie I'm Pete and this is Valerie. Derek and Rose are a lovely couple, we have so much in common. We will be keeping in touch when we leave"

'I bet you will' thought Ellie.

"Yes they said they were entertaining you in their room after the gin tour and that you made quite a night of it"

"Yes that's right, very hospitable couple; we were up 'til dawn I believe and just slept where we dropped. We were all going on the same trips the next day so we all went together. You should join us for the next party, I'm sure you would be more than welcome." Offered Pete, with a little too much of a lecherous smile.

"Um...yes...maybe ..I would have to ask the boss you know..haha...well it was nice talking to you both" Ellie piled her plate with chicken pakora and chips and almost ran back to the table.

"What's wrong with you Elle? You look like you've seen a ghost" asked Aggie concerned by how pale she was.

"No I'm ok....I think I've just been invited to a swinger's party though..."

"Really? Where? When?" asked Peggy as she looked around excitedly.

"Margaret don't you dare!" exclaimed Aggie affronted.

"What? I wasn't wanting to go, I'm just curious as to what goes on..."

"Why am I always here for these conversations? This is why I'm going to need therapy I'm sure of it" muttered Kate as she looked at her Aunt who smiled back cheekily.

"Apart from that, it appears that Derek and Rose have an alibi. They were 'entertaining' all night and then were with the same people up until they left for their tour. They wouldn't have had time to kill him.

"At least that narrows it down a little" said Kate and then she grinned "Was I invited to this party too?" she said with a wink.

"I don't know, I think it was my charm and good looks that got me the invite" said Ellie grinning as she ducked the napkin that was swatted at her arm.

CHAPTER 13

◆ ◆ ◆

T he next morning Ellie woke with a start when she heard a loud thump. She sat bolt upright in bed and tried to look through the darkness, she fumbled for the light and flicked the switch. She found Kate on the floor rubbing her left leg with tears running down her cheeks.

"Honey what happened?! Are you ok? She leapt from the bed and took Kate's hands to gently lift her from the floor. She sat her on the bed and had a look at her leg.

"I'm fine Ellie, my leg just went from under me when I was going for some water. I must have been walking too much recently, I should have been using my stick more."

"Does it hurt? Is there anything I can do?" Ellie asked wishing above all else that she could take this pain from Kate.

"It hurts but there's nothing we can do about it, I'm just going to have to rest it a bit more." Kate wiped tears away impatiently, she hated crying.
"Well todays trip is a coach tour around Rome, no walking involved so at least that will help." Ellie tried to cheer her up, she knew Kate had been looking forward to seeing Rome.

"Are you coming on the trip?" Kate asked hopefully

"No, I'm sorry honey I need to call Gavin and get more information but your mum and Peggy will be with you and trust me there are no better bodyguards in the world. I'll have my phone with me so you can video chat whenever you get time. If I get this stuff done today then I can go to Pompeii tomorrow."

"OK, that seems a fair trade. You're right, this trip will be easier on me than walking around this ship all day would be. I'll bring you back a present"

"So long as you come back in one piece and not too tired then I'll be happy." Ellie smiled and so did Kate. Ellie had been gently massaging the muscles in Kate's leg to try to get them relaxed. She could feel the spasms underneath her fingers and knew that Kate was hurting more than she let on.

"Do you want me to grab you some breakfast so you can eat here and rest until you need to go?" Kate nodded happily "That would be lovely, just a coffee and some pancakes would be perfect."

"Consider it done" Ellie pulled on a pair of shorts and a t-shirt, slipped into her trainers and headed to the breakfast buffet before the hordes arrived. She returned within 10 mins with a tray full of pancakes, French toast, coffee and orange juice.

"You're an angel" groaned Kate as she grabbed a coffee and some French toast.

"Don't spread that rumour around, I've got a reputation to uphold" Ellie smiled as she picked up her own coffee and switched on the news. They were making their way through the stack of pancakes when Kate suddenly pointed at the tv

"Ellie turn it up!"

"What's wrong" asked Ellie alarmed as she fumbled for the remote to turn it up. The news anchor was reading a story about the national fiction awards and that the nominees were being announced.

"Sorry I didn't mean to scare you, I just wanted to see this. My publisher has a few authors up for nomination in several categories so I want to see who gets the nod."

"Ah ok, are you one of them?"

"No, I'm nowhere near as recognised as these people will be, maybe someday though."

"So what, you're new book is in the best seller list. That must mean something."

The newsreader cut to the video feed of the live nominations. The head of the National Fiction Authors Association was reading out the nominees. Kate recognised the people up for best romance novel and best thriller and was genuinely pleased for their achievements. Next up was the crime author award.

"The nominees are; Laura Martin for 'The stalker', James Crow for 'Strangled at dawn', Eric Steinberg for 'The Nazi killer' and finally Katherine Mitchell for 'Murder on the Clyde'.

Both sat silent for a second and then Ellie let up a loud whoop "You did it!! That is so amazing!! I'm so so proud of you Kate!" she picked her up and swung her round planting a kiss on the smaller woman who was still stunned into silence.

"That...that can't be right...my publisher never said that I was being considered. Why wouldn't she tell me that? Oh god I'm going to need to go to an awards dinner....will you come with me? I won't be half as nervous if you're there."

"Of course, it would be an honour to escort you m'lady" Ellie bowed and Kate laughed at her antics.

"On second thoughts, if you're going to be all dorky about it I might take my mum instead." Ellie mimed pulling the knife out of her heart and staggered backwards to the bed. "So....cold..... come closer" she pulled Kate to her and pulled her into a huge hug. "I'm proud of you, and I promise I'll be on my best behaviour, brownies honour."

"You were in the brownies?" Kate asked dubiously

"Yes...well for about two weeks. My mum and dad forked out for the uniform and then I decided I didn't like it. They were furious, but it still counts right?"

"It does, we better get dressed. If I don't tell mum first she will be in an official huff for the rest of the holiday" Kate warned as she got off the bed and started pulling clothes out.

When they got to Aggie and Peggy's cabin the door was flung open and Aggie launched herself at her daughter and pulled her into a huge hug.

"Oh Katie I can't believe it! Why didn't you tell us that you were up for nomination?" Aggie was crying as she stopped hugging Kate and allowed Peggy to give her niece a hug.

"I didn't know mum, honestly I knew nothing about it. I just found out because it was on the news. I'll need to call my publisher when we get back today and find out details."

"I think a celebration is in order! I say we go to the al la carte restaurant tonight for dinner" suggested Aggie

"Mum we are going there tomorrow for your birthday, how about we just have a meal and maybe watch the entertainment in the lounge tonight and then we have a posh meal tomorrow instead?"

"Are you sure? It's not every day you get award nominations Katie, I get a birthday every year." Aggie said

"No, birthday meals are important, I don't want you to miss

yours." They hadn't told Aggie that they had planned a cake to be presented by the staff. It was a surprise that Peggy had arranged when they had arrived.

"Girls look at the time, we need to get going! Our coach is due to leave soon." announced Peggy as she looked at her watch.

"I'll walk down with you, I need to head to my new office and call Gavin." said Ellie as she shouldered her backpack containing her laptop.

"You're not coming to Rome? Oh Ellie are you sure? It's going to be a wonderful tour." said Aggie with disappointment in her tone.

"Sorry Aggie, I need to do a few things on board today, I won't get the chance tomorrow if we are out at Pompeii. Just take some nice pictures for me and tell me all about it tonight."

They walked down the stairs to the deck 4 disembarkation area, Ellie hugged them all and kissed Kate goodbye. She watched them get on their coach and then turned back towards the ship. She caught up with Jen on her way and had a brainwave.

"Jen, could you give me a list of everyone that was on the gin tour with you?"
"Of course, here" Jen handed Ellie a piece of paper from her clip board. "I usually keep them all together until the end of the cruise." Jen explained

"Thanks a lot Jen, that's a great help for me" Ellie said before making her way to the library.

The library had a sign posted on the door that it was closed for the duration of the voyage. Ellie opened the door and headed towards the desk where she set up her laptop and connected it to the modem situated under the desk. She called Gavin to see if he had got any useful information.

"Hey boss lady, is your better half there? I want to say congrats,

I saw the news this morning. You must be proud of her eh?" said Gavin beaming into the camera.

"I am proud, sadly she's not here right now, she's off on a coach tour of Rome but I'll tell her you said congrats."

"Why aren't you also on a tour of Rome Els?"

"I need to sort some of this out Gav, there is no way I would be able to enjoy the sights with all of this spinning around in my head."

"Els for Christ sake you're supposed to be on holiday. I know you're rusty at this but I'm pretty sure it entails seeing some nice buildings and sitting in the sun drinking cocktails."

"Yes I know, I don't need a lecture thanks. If I get some things sorted today I can enjoy tomorrow. Pompeii is a place I've always wanted to see so believe me I won't miss that."

"Ok, I'll forgive you this time" he smiled sweetly

"You're all heart. Do you have anything for me on the Major?"

"I'm fine, thanks for asking." Gavin replied sarcastically. Ellie rolled her eyes and was about to reply but Gavin held up his hands in surrender

"I do, hang on until I get the information up in front of me. He clicked a few pages open on his computer and started reading aloud from them.

"Edward Charleston was born in Glasgow in 1952. His family were a military family, his father and 3 of his uncles fought in the war. His father was in the RAF and the uncles were in the Navy. They are an affluent family too; his great grandfather was a Lord Hamish Charleston. He was a conservative politician who fought against unionisation of workers."

"Charming" muttered Ellie.

"Aye, so not much is known about Major Charleston, he joined up when he was 18 and he retired 5 years ago. He owns one of those large Georgian houses off Great Western Road, he lives alone and has never married. His military record is sealed Ellie, I've tried all my contacts but no one can get access to it. The only thing we have is that he served in Northern Ireland in the 70s and was involved in the first Gulf War campaign in some capacity. There are no details on anything he did or even what Regiment he served in."

"That's frustrating, keep trying for more on his career. If it's sealed then there's obviously a story behind it. Have you anything else on him?"

"He was arrested for drink driving 4 years ago but the case was dismissed due to lack of evidence. The officers didn't get to breath test him at the scene, he had already made it home and his solicitor said he took a drink once he got home. There was no way to prove he didn't. Since he retired he seems to spend his time either on the golf course or doing talks on wine tasting. That's all I've got Els."

"It's not much to go on, his drink driving charge, did he hit anyone?"

"No, he was parking the car at home but kept missing the entrance to his driveway and pranged a few cars out on the main road. A neighbour called the police as the Major got out of the car and tried to take a penalty kick at her cat. He missed and landed on his arse in the road." Gavin explained. "The neighbour was a Mrs Kent, she's 83 and lives alone."

Ellie sighed, she was hoping for more. There didn't seem to be much in the Major's life. She felt certain the answer could lie in his military record.

"Good work Gavin, keep working on that military record. I'll see what I can find out on this end. I've confirmed a couple of alibis but there are still a few possible suspects I need to chase down today. Thanks for this Gav"

"It's what I'm here for, besides if I'm helping you then I look busy so I don't get stuck doing the paperwork." He responded cheerfully. "I'll keep working on this Els don't worry. Now you make sure to give Kate a big hug from me and for god sake, try to do some actual holiday stuff tomorrow."

"I'll try, talk to you soon." She hung up and sat for a moment trying to decide what to do next. She used the library phone to call up reception and get transferred to the Captain. He had checked the rotas and confirmed that Jen was on the early shift with her roommate and that she had indeed been on the excursion help desk once she returned from the gin tour. Ellie crossed off Jen from her suspect list. She decided to try to track down some of the others from the gin tour list. She got up and headed back out to look for either the Welsh couple, the Americans or their majesties.

Kate was on the coach enjoying the sights of Rome, she was sad that Ellie couldn't be there to share it with her though. She was lost in her own thoughts as they were stopped in front of a government building when she heard a woman talking behind her.

"..did you notice that woman going around and asking questions yesterday? These lesbians are all the same, bossy and interfering. Who does she think she is? I mean it's bad enough that these freaks are allowed on this cruise with us normal folk but to then start marching around asking questions? It's too much honestly. I've noticed they aren't on this trip that I can see so at least our day won't be polluted by seeing them cavorting around. Disgusting"

Kate was shaking with rage. She was small enough that they hadn't noticed her sitting in front of them. She was about to turn round and put whoever it was in their place when she felt a hand grabbing her arm. Peggy had leaned across the aisle and was trying to calm her niece while also pinning Aggie to her seat on the opposite side. They had obviously heard the conversation too. Peggy shook her head at her in warning. Kate got the message, if she mouthed off it would put whoever it was on their guard and that wouldn't help Ellie. Kate took a deep breath and nodded to Peggy that she was ok. Aggie was still attempting to get out of her seat but Peggy was stronger and kept her pinned. Peggy then whispered to Aggie and Aggie eventually settled down. Peggy then wrote a note on her phone and passed it to Kate.

'It's the Queen behind you, don't argue with her. Let her think that Ellie is just being nosey. If they find out the truth then they will be on their guard even more around her. We can punch her later.'

Kate smiled and nodded her understanding. They were due to stop for a walk and some lunch soon, she felt that distance between her mother and the vile women behind her would be the best thing right now.

Ellie was walking the decks, she needed to profile this killer but lacked the information she needed. She started piecing together what she had in her mind. This kill was personal which would mean they knew the Major. There was no way that they could know he was to be on this trip so they didn't come here with the intention of killing him but the plan was put in place quickly, probably during the gin tour and the mention of the almond gin. The killer had to know enough about the Major to know about the allergy too. This is someone from his past. Ellie was sure the service record would be important in finding the link.

As Ellie rounded the corner she spotted the Americans huddled over a vent near the shopping area. They spotted her and straightened up quickly and headed in the opposite direction before she could call out to them. Ellie walked over to the vent and looked to see what they were doing. There were definite toll marks around the edges and on the screws keeping the vent in place. 'What the hell are those two doing?'

The Pope was doing a mass at St Peter's so there were crowds of people everywhere as Kate, Peggy and Aggie made their way through the square towards a café. As they waited on their lunch order Kate spots a little gift shop beside the café and decides to find an appropriate gift for Ellie. She is looking at the display shelves inside and she spots a little model of the Colosseum that she knew Ellie would love. She was just about to go to the till to pay for it when she heard the Queen just outside the doorway. Kate peeked out and saw that she was seated at a table at a café on the other side of the shop to where Peggy and Aggie were.

"I didn't know that Lizzie, why didn't you ever tell me?" it was the Queen Mother speaking.

"I just assumed you knew, none of us have changed that much in 40 years Bridie but I don't want to talk about it. Today is a happy day, the sun is shining and we are in the most beautiful city in the world so let's enjoy it"

"But Lizzie..."

"No! I won't discuss it!" the Queen warned.

Kate was hidden in the doorway trying to listen to the full conversation but she was interrupted by the shop owner speaking angrily in rapid Italian. It would appear that he thought Kate was trying to steal the statue in her hands. She muttered an apology and handed over 20 euros and left the shop quickly while avoiding the notice of the ladies outside. She needed to tell Ellie what she had overheard as soon as she got back.

Kate relayed the conversation to her mum and aunt as they walked back to the coach. She hadn't seen the Queen look that happy during the entire trip and it worried her. They stopped to take some pictures of the piazza and spotted a large army truck parked at the edge of the fountain. The Queen was just ahead of them and she took a picture of the Queen Mother or Bridie as Kate now knew her name to be, beside the truck. A young soldier came darting towards them with a machine gun and snatched the phone off them and was in the process of deleting it. The Queen looked irate. As they passed Peggy picked up what the soldier was shouting in Italian.

"You aren't allowed to take pictures of service army personal on duty." Peggy explained once they had past the drama. They boarded the coach quickly and noticed that the Queen was in a powerful mood when she finally boarded the coach. She sat down at the back and refused to look at or speak to anyone for the duration of the trip back to the ship.

Ellie had finally tracked down the Welsh couple, she didn't know why she hadn't thought of it before, the gym! She found both of them in there lifting heavy weights.

"Hello there Ellie, we've not seen you around here before. Do you need a hand on any of the equipment?" asked Barbara as she set down some dumbbells.

"No I'm fine, I'm just here to look around and check out the facilities. How are you both? Did you hear about the Major?" she decided to just go straight for it.

"Yes we heard; I would like to say I was sorry about his death but I'm not. He was a bully and I don't think the world will miss him" explained Owain as he continued his reps with the weights.

"I don't think many people will miss him, he wasn't well liked. Do you come up here often?"

"Yes we are here most of the time, if we aren't booked on any excursions you can find us here most evenings." Said Barbara

"I might need to get Aggie and Peggy up here, after the gin cruise they were so drunk they had to be carried to bed. Where you two in a similar state that night?" Ellie asked lightly.

"Oh no, we rarely drink to excess. There are too many calories involved in a binge, but we tried the gin on the day. We worked it off that night though, there was a spin class on and we did that followed by a 10k run on the treadmill. We were exhausted after that; we went to bed early as we were on the early excursion the next day."

Ellie looked at her watch and made her excuses to leave saying she had to meet Kate in 10 mins. As she left she looked at the notice board, it detailed all the classes on at the gym and there was a spin class that lasted 2 hours that evening. She noticed a cctv camera overhead too. If she watched that and checked out their alibi it would help. She figured that as the Major had been in his pyjamas, the gin had to have been placed in his room before he went to bed that night. She doubted there would have been time for them to have set it up if they had been at the gym most of the night.

Ellie was waiting in the lounge bar when Kate Aggie and Peggy arrived back.

"What's up Ellie, you look like someone's kicked your puppy" asked Peggy as she sat down at the table.

"Oh nothing, I'm just frustrated by a lack of information. The Major's service record is sealed, I can't get any information other than he served in Northern Ireland. I have a feeling that there's something in there that could help." Ellie became quiet again. Peggy got her phone out and dialled a number, as she got up to take the call she said to Ellie

"Leave it with me, I'll see what I can do."

Kate, Ellie and Aggie watched as Peggy made a quick and almost silent call, they only picked up the Major's name in the conversation before she hung up and returned to the table.

"You will have the unsealed record within 24 hours Ellie, a colleague will be emailing it to you."

Ellie sat dumbfounded, just how much influence did Peggy have?

CHAPTER 14

◆ ◆ ◆

T he next morning they woke to the sound of grinding gears coming from outside.

"What the hell is that noise?" mumbled Kate from under the duvet.

"I've no idea, hang on I'll take a look"

Ellie scrambled out of bed and opened the curtains to find the view obscured by a large white mass descending past the window. She was momentarily confused until she saw the name of the ship stamped on the side.

"It's the lifeboats" explained Ellie as she crawled back to bed.

"Are we sinking?!" asked Kate slightly alarmed but still speaking from under the duvet.

"If we are, they're keeping it a secret." Mumbled Ellie as she tried to go back to sleep.

Just then the tannoy crackled to life

"Oh bugger off with the announcements" grumbled Kate

"Good morning ladies and gents it's the voice from the ceiling and welcome to sunny Sorrento! Now some of you may have noticed that the crew are in the process of lowering the lifeboats. Don't panic, we aren't sinking ha ha ha. The port at Sorrento is too shallow for us to take the ship any closer so we have to transport you ashore via the lifeboats. It will be an adventure and you can all do your Kate and Leo impressions on the journey"

"If he thinks I'm hanging off the end of a floating door and freezing to death he's got a strange interpretation of the word 'adventure'" grumbled Kate as she got up and stretched her stiff muscles. The tannoy continued;

"The lifeboats will be available all throughout the day for anyone wishing to go ashore and see the sights on their own but if you are booked on any coach excursions we would ask that you are ashore before 10am in order to get to you allocated coaches. The weather is sunny and clear for the day with highs of 35C so please make sure you have plenty of water with you. On behalf of the Captain and the crew we hope you enjoy your day and we hope to see you this evening in our various restaurants and shows." The bing bong of the xylophone was followed by crackling and the tannoy announcement was over.

Kate was grabbing clothes for after her shower as Ellie called room service and ordered breakfast to be brought up to their cabin. She also ordered a special birthday breakfast to be delivered to Aggie and Peggy's cabin too.

"Are you going to be able to go today or do you have stuff to do?" Kate asked

"There's nothing much I can do until Peggy's contact comes back with that record or Gavin finds anything else. Most of our suspects will be offshore today too so I may as well enjoy the trip and keep an eye on them at the same time."

"Oh speaking of that, I totally forgot to tell you what I overheard yesterday" said Kate, she went on to explain the conversation she overheard between the Queen and Queen Mother or Liz and Bridie as she now knew them to be called. Ellie listened with a frown on her face and then began pacing. She was interrupted by the arrival of their breakfast. Once they were alone again she continued her pacing now with a piece of toast.

"Why would they care what I'm doing if they aren't involved? There is definitely something going on with those two, I'll try to keep my eye on them today I think."

They met Aggie and Peggy in the queue for the lifeboats and both gave big hugs to birthday girl Aggie who was sporting a very large and gaudy birthday badge.

"She made me wear it" explained Aggie as she glared at a thoroughly pleased Peggy. "Thank you for my breakfast girls, it was lovely to not have to get up. They were helped onto the lifeboat by the deck hands and found seats near the back. The Queen and Queen Mother were perched on the back bench glaring at Derek, Rose and their friends. Owain and Barbara were at the other side of the boat and waved as they sat down. Peggy was already looking decidedly green around the gills as the lifeboat rocked up and down to the motion of the waves.

The boat moves off at speed and bounces over the waves towards Sorrento. The town was perched on top of a cliff, there were steps built in to the cliff from the sea.

"I hope they aren't expecting us to hike all the way up there?" complained the Queen

"Actually I believe there is a dock further round for us to get ashore, no steps involved dear lady" said Derek cheerfully. The Queen looked at him like he was something she had scraped off her shoe and turned her back on him.

"Such a rude woman" muttered Aggie staring daggers into the

back of her head.

The boat finally arrived at the dock and they were helped up the steps and offered fruit punch as they waited in line for their tour. A very tanned older man in white shorts, a white cap and a bright green ascot came bounding up to them. He introduced himself as Salvatore their tour guide for Pompeii.

"Ladies and gentlemen if you would follow me please, we need to get you on the coaches now." He held up a paddle with tour number 25 on it and herded everyone through the busy portside towards a carpark filled with minibuses. He counted everyone on board the air conditioned bus only briefly held up by the Queen complaining about how far she had to walk already.

"Why is she coming on this tour if she doesn't want to walk? What does she think is waiting for her in Pompeii? Does she think she's getting carried about like Cleopatra?" grumbled Peggy

Once everyone was settled the bus took off like a scalded cat. The roads around Sorrento were narrow and winding, the bus driver did not seem to notice as he took hairpin bends at 60 miles an hour narrowly dodging a moped driver and an old woman who was carrying water. Aggie hand her hands over her eyes and was swearing like a docker. Peggy was thoroughly enjoying the crazy driving and was giggling like a teenager as she watched frightened tourists diving out of the way of this runaway bus. They made their way up the hill and finally reached a coach park where the driver slammed the brakes on so hard that poor Rose, who had been sitting in the middle of the back row, was thrown off her seat and skidded down the aisle. Ellie rushed to help her to her feet.

"Thank Ellie, it's been a while since I've had carpet burns like that on my knees" she gave Ellie a cheeky wink and then went back to her seat leaving Ellie speechless.

Everyone got off the bus and Salvatore led them to a much larger coach that would take them the rest of the way to Pompeii. Aggie looked dubious; Ellie knew she was thinking about the huge coach and the tiny winding streets they had already encountered. The coach took them along the beautiful mountain road out of Sorrento. Ellie and Kate watched the scenery out the window, below them was the beautiful Amalfi coast and several large cruise liners anchored at sea. They then travelled through several tunnels and at last arrived at the ancient city of Pompeii. Salvatore led them like ants towards the entrance to the archaeological site. Kate was in her element, she took a few pictures of Mount Vesuvius in the background as they waited to go in.

Salvatore got all their tickets sorted and quickly led them up the long pathway to towards the amphitheatre and the excavated streets beyond. He pointed out the original tiles and pipe work in the roman baths, Ellie was in awe of the beauty of the stonework inside. They walked through the cobblestone streets taking in all the beautiful statues and the houses of people long gone. They were walking up a long narrow street when Peggy nudged Ellie mischievously and pointed to something above a doorway beside them. Salvatore spotted her action.

"Ah yes Senora you have spotted a bit of advertising Pompeii style! If you would direct your attention ladies and gentlemen to the symbol above this doorway, note the shape. It is a phallic symbol yes? This is how the locals advertised the brothel. If you look inside these rooms you will see stone beds in each one and if you follow me in here you will see that the original wall decorations have survived too."

They walked in to find the ancient roman equivalent of the Kama Sutra painted on the walls. Peggy started snapping pictures of all the paintings as Kate wandered around looking at them. She found one of two young men and smiled, she showed it to Ellie. She heard a tut behind her as she turned to see the Queen looking horrified at the images.

"Filth, absolute filth, is it any wonder these disgusting people had to kill Jesus" and then she marched off ahead.

"Did she seriously just say that?" asked an astonished Ellie. "Does she know anything about ancient Rome? Why in hell did she come here if she is just going to be so snooty and judgemental?"

Kate continued to wander around, Ellie watched her. Kate seemed so happy to be there, taking in the history of a place that died so long ago. Derek, Rose and their friends were studying one of the mosaics very closely, Ellie grinned when she noticed that it was an image depicting a Roman orgy.

The couple with matching moustaches and very loud floral shirts had also found the image of the two men and were giggling loudly as they tried to mimic the position but ended up falling over each other instead. Ellie offered to take their picture with the image and they happily posed with it as they hugged each other lovingly.

"Thanks love, there's no way we could have passed up seeing this. Not on our honeymoon anyway" the taller man beamed.

"Oh, congratulations!" Ellie said warmly as she shook their hands.

"Thanks love, how long have you and your good lady been married?"

"We aren't, well not yet anyway. I'm um....I'm working up to it" Ellie replied quietly as she looked around to make sure Kate wasn't in earshot.

"Oooh a proposal, how are you going to do it?"

"Have you got the ring?"

"Do you have the perfect location?"

These questions were fired at her quickly by the couple and she panicked.

"I....um....I hadn't really got that far. I've only just got the courage up to make the decision" Ellie had gone pale and hadn't realised she had stop talking until the smaller of the two men patted her hand sympathetically.

"Don't panic love, no matter how or when you ask, she'll say yes" he said confidently.

"I wish I was as sure as you are, but thank you, you're both very kind"

"I'm sure only because I'm watching how she looks at you love, she loves you very much. It's clear in her eyes" he said simply. Ellie turned to see Kate watching her from across the room. Her eyes were bright and her smile loving. Ellie returned it and sighed happily.

"Where are our manners, my name is Kenny and this is my husband Sidney" said the smaller man"

"Nice to meet you, I'm Ellie and that is Kate over there" she said as she pointed to Kate who was now attempting to prize Peggy away from a rather detailed mosaic. It must have been good; Peggy had put her reading glasses on.

The tour continued back outside, the afternoon sun was beating down and it was very warm to be walking about. Kate had started to slow down a bit, the heat had used up all of her energy and she was beginning to fatigue but she was determined to see everything. She carried on with a slower gait and a slight limp. They get taken to a large open area surrounded by temples, pillars and statues to the various gods. Ellie was taking a picture of the others beside a bust of Apollo and Diana when she spotted the Queen and Queen mother having an argument in the background. She was too far away to hear what was said but the Queen looked furious, she was pointing and gesticulating in a menacing way as the Queen mother had her hands up to placate her friend. What was it with those two?

Salvatore led them back out to the refreshment area and told them they had 45 minutes to have something to eat or buy gifts before they were due back to the coach. As none of them were particularly hungry, they walked up and down through the souvenir stalls. Ellie and Kate bought a statue of the cast of one of Vesuvius victims. Aggie thought it was a bit macabre but Ellie agreed with Kate that it truly symbolised the disaster that met these people. They purchased some small gifts for people back home, Ellie found a gladiator statue for Gavin and then they found a bench to rest at while Ellie grabbed cold drinks from a street vendor. Aggie and Peggy returned carrying two heavy bags but they refused to say what they had bought. Ellie took a peak in the bags when they weren't looking; they had bought stone replicas of the symbol outside the brothel. Classy thought Ellie with a grin.

CHAPTER 15

◆ ◆ ◆

The journey back to the ship was even more death defying as the one to leave. With all the winding roads now on a downhill slant, the driver took no notice of the increasing speed as he hurtled round corners so fast that Peggy actually smacked her head against the window, as she was peeling her cheek from the pane she noticed an old woman not 6 inches from the window shaking a loaf of bread at the bus and a cyclist that had leaped off his bike and into a hedge.

The bus slammed the brakes hard and they screeched into the carpark narrowly missing the bus in front of them. Aggie and Peggy shakily walked off the bus, pale and swearing. Rose was blowing into a paper bag held by Derek as he shouted at the driver who couldn't understand English so was therefore unaffected by the rant. The Queen and Queen Mother got off and demanded wheelchairs back to the ship. It was explained to them that the lifeboat was a mere 20 yards away and therefore it would take longer to order the chairs than it would take for them to slowly walk there.

"I don't care if it takes you longer, I want a chair. I'm entitled to one after dragging us all over some ruined rocks all day. Get us the chairs, we'll wait"

She sat down at a bench and that was the final word.

"Good to see that she enjoyed the trip eh?" Ellie said to Kate.

"Why come? What did she think was going to happen on a walk around an archaeological site?" said Kate as she glared at the woman. She was in pain, her leg had started to get heavy during the trip but she carried on through the pain and fatigue as best she could. Kate wouldn't have asked for a chair even if her leg was dragging behind her, not for 20 yards. She had noticed that the Queen was sprightly when walking and never showed any ounce of pain during any of the trips. She would never assume someone wasn't disabled as not all disabilities are visible, but it appeared to her that the woman only ever requested this assistance when she wanted a bit of extra attention from the staff.

They walked slowly back towards the lifeboats, Kate holding on to Ellie's arm a little more than she would normally in order to give herself a bit more balance. Aggie and Peggy had regained some of their colour from the bus trip of death and were chatting away about the different pictures they had taken and Aggie was looking in her gift bag and giggling.

The trip back on the lifeboat was quick; they had been the last passengers to get on this particular boat before it left. As they were pulling away they spotted the Queen getting pushed towards the dock in her chair and watched as she started gesticulating angrily at having missed the boat. Kate grinned evilly as she knew there would be a half hour wait for the next one to depart.

Back on board the ship Aggie and Peggy decided that they needed a lie down after their adventures of the day and agreed to meet up later for Aggie's birthday dinner. Kate took advantage of this time to also have a sleep as Ellie tried to get in touch with Gavin. He didn't answer so she assumed he must be busy at work so she settled down and went over the timeline again to see if she could make sense of the Major's death. There were a few questions that were bugging her; how did the killer get into his room? How did they know about his nut allergy? How did they know to disguise the gin as water as the Major wouldn't have touched it otherwise?

Ellie started to note down possible scenarios, they could have asked the steward to be allowed entry to the room or possibly given the gin to him to put in the room for them. She noted that she should check to see if the lock had been tampered with and to bring Peggy with her for her expertise in this area.

The nut allergy they could possibly have worked out the same way Kate eventually did or, more likely, the killer knew the Major and therefore knew of it beforehand. This would also explain how they knew to disguise the gin. She was convinced this had to be someone from the Major's past. It was the only way this made sense to her. She looked over to check on Kate who was fast asleep, Ellie got up and left the room quietly, she wanted to track down the steward to find out if he had indeed let anyone in.

She found him very quickly as he was down the corridor delivering drinks to a cabin, she caught up with him as he left the cabin.

"Hi Eddie, are you busy?" Eddie stopped and smiled a little uneasily at her

"No Madam I'm not too busy, how can I help you?

"I just have a couple of questions for you concerning the day of the Major's death. Did you let anyone into his room that day?"

Eddie blanched and replied "Oh no Madam, that is completely against our rules. The only time we are allowed to do this is if the person is an occupant of that cabin and do not have their key on them."

"Did anyone ever ask you to let them in?"

"No Madam"

"Ok, did anyone give you the water jug to put in the Major's cabin?"

Eddie thought for a moment and then shook his head.

"No Madam, I did not place any water jug in his cabin. We only replace bottled water in the cabins. I had assumed the Major had brought it with him from one of the bars" explained Eddie.

"I see, thank you Eddie that's been a help to me" said Ellie as she started back towards her cabin.

"Madam...there...there was a note left on my cart the day before. I do not know if it is relevant but it was certainly strange as it concerned the Major."

"Go ahead Eddie, what was the note?"

"It was a note, supposedly from the Major, asking me to not disturb him by coming in for the morning cleaning. I thought it strange; it did not seem to be the Major's hand writing. He had signed many receipts for wine in his room over the course of the voyage and he always used a black fountain pen that he carried with him and his writing was scrawled like the way a Doctor's would be?" Ellie nodded as he continued "well the note was in blue biro ink and the handwriting was block letters and quite light on the paper. I don't know if that means anything Madam but I thought it strange" Eddie looked embarrassed as he tailed off his explanation.

"Eddie, that's been really helpful thank you. Do you still have this note?" she asked hopefully.

"No I'm sorry Madam; it was thrown out with the rubbish at the end of my shift."

"I presume that you did as the note instructed in that you did not go in for the morning clean?"

"No I did not. I waited until the evening turn down service before I entered his cabin and that's when I found him..." Eddie tailed off again as he relived the moment of finding the body.

"Eddie if anything else comes to you, come and find me. You've been so helpful." Ellie shook his hand with warmth and he even managed a relieved smile before he hurried off towards the bar again.

The Griffin restaurant was beautifully decorated in an art deco style. The tables lined the walls and had a beautiful view of the Italian coast as lights twinkled in the distance and the sun was setting. They had all dressed up for Aggie's birthday and they brought gifts and cards with them for her to open.

Aggie was in a brand new navy blue dress that brought out the colour of her eyes. She happily accepted the birthday cards and read each one slowly; she loved reading the words in a card. Peggy presented her with a large bottle of gin with strict instructions for it not to be consumed until they were home.

"We've got that show to go to at the Pavilion theatre next month so I think that would be the perfect night for it" Peggy explained as Kate snorted into her drink earning her a glare from her aunt.

"A show? Aunt Peggy it's that dodgy hypnotist that makes people simulate sex and do obscene things with fruit that you're going to, not the Opera"

Sensing an argument about to break out, Ellie decided it was time to hand over her own gift for Aggie. She had given Aggie a beautiful picture frame containing a black and white picture of her with Kate. Ellie had taken the picture in the summer when they had all went on a picnic. They were both laughing at something and holding on to each other, their eyes crinkled in laughter. Ellie loved the picture of mother and daughter. Aggie looked at it and her eyes shone. She got up to hug Ellie and whispered her thanks in her ear.

Kate handed over her gift and a separate envelope, the gift was a beautiful watch that she had ordered from Argyle Arcade in Glasgow. It had her own and Aggie's birthstones around the face. Aggie was thrilled with it and put it on immediately as she admired the gemstones twinkling in the light. She then turned her attention towards the envelope, she opened it up and read the simple piece of paper slowly. Kate and Ellie smiled as Aggie started bouncing in her seat excitedly.

"You're taking me to the awards dinner that you've been nominated in?! Oh Kate that is wonderful, I'll need to find an outfit" she stopped and then looked at Ellie "Oh Ellie, surely it's your place to go to this?" Ellie stopped her quickly

"No Aggie, this is Kate's first award and it's only right that you should be there. This is a big deal and you've always been Kate's biggest supporter. It's your place to go." Ellie said emphatically and she squeezed Kate's hand. They had discussed it earlier and Ellie had insisted on it.

The meal was beautiful and they spent a long time enjoying the scenery and the flavours. They were chatting as they waited for the desert course and as Aggie was talking to Kate about different fabrics for a dress, Ellie noticed Peggy's face twitching into a grin. Ellie tracked Peggy's eyes and instantly knew what was amusing her. Ellie kicked Kate under the table and silently motioned for her to look behind Aggie as she herself tried to stifle a laugh. Aggie noticed none of this as she was still chatting about the awards dinner. It wasn't until the first strums of the guitar were heard behind her that she froze. She didn't have to turn around to know that this was for her; the three manic grins that faced her were enough to confirm the worst.

A full mariachi band surrounded the table along with the majority of the restaurant staff as they presented her with a birthday cake and started to serenade her with a birthday song. Peggy was in her element as Aggie's face turned crimson and she tried to slink down under the table. The band were unfazed as they bent low to catch her eye as they continued to sing to her. Ellie was filming all this as she laughed. Finally the band finished their song and then got the entire restaurant to also sing 'Happy Birthday' to Aggie before they let her blow the candles out and make a wish. Peggy thanked the staff and the band as Aggie busied herself cutting the cake.

"Peggy I may kill you before this trip is over" she said as she handed her sister a huge slice of cake.

At the end of the evening Kate and Ellie entered their cabin and slumped on the couch full from their meal and a sumptuous chocolate cake that Aggie had taken back to her room with her. Kate switched on the tv as she started to get changed for bed and Ellie opened her laptop to check her emails.

"Finally! I've got the email about the Major's service record!" she was excited as she clicked open the attached files and started to read as Kate sat down beside her to read too.

"Ok he served in the Paras during the 1970s and was based in Belfast between 1972 and 1976. He seemed well regarded by his commanding officer and was put forward for promotion in 1973 and again in 1975. There was an accusation of heavy handed tactics from his division but this was investigated at the time and nothing was found. Oh look at this, there's a personal note from his Captain regarding his departure from Northern Ireland in 1976. The Captain states that his removal so suddenly was for his own personal safety and for the safety of the rest of the regiment. He had been spotted taking a local catholic girl out on the town for several months before, the girl got pregnant. The IRA found out and was threatening retaliation for this treachery on both him and the girl."

"That's awful" whispered Kate as Ellie continued to read

"It gets worse look, the girl's family were targeted after the Major was shipped out. Her dad was murdered by a shot to the back of the head on waste ground behind their house, her brother was blown up in a car bomb two months later and her mother was given a bullet to the knee in her own kitchen a day after the funeral of her husband."

"My god, what happened to the girl?" said Kate with tears in her eyes as she thought of so much suffering happening to one family.

"Not much is known but the Captain has noted that she left Northern Ireland for her own safety and they believed she settled in Scotland. They have her name as Mary Rankin but that she had since changed it for her own protection as the IRA were still looking for her in Scotland."

This was it, Ellie was sure of it. This had to be the reason that the Major was killed!

CHAPTER 16

◆ ◆ ◆

T he next morning Ellie tried to reach Gavin and, again, got nothing. She sent a quick message to him asking him to check the system for a Mary Rankin who moved to Scotland around 1976. She wanted to know what she had changed her name to and any other information he could find on her as quickly as possible. Ellie had discussed the file with Peggy and she agreed to ask her contacts for any information they could find on her too.

Today they were docked in Sicily and were booked on a trip to ancient Segesta. Ellie decided to go as she could do nothing more until she heard from Gavin. She had thought of who could possibly have been involved in this business from 1976. The Queen or Queen Mother looked like they could have been the right age to be Mary Rankin but she also thought of Jen; she was the right age to be the child caught in the middle of that mess. She also thought of Kenny, the smaller man from the couple she had met in Pompeii, he was younger than his husband and could easily have been the right age. She also remembered Peggy telling her about the Queen glaring at him during the pub quiz. Peggy had assumed it was blatant homophobia but what if it was much more than that? She hadn't thought to check his alibi as he had not been on the gin tour but his mother may have told him about his father and his allergy at some point in his life.

She continued mulling this over in her head until they boarded the coach and met their driver Mario and their guide Maria. Once again the Queen and Queen mother had ditched their chairs and were sat at the front of the coach. They glared at Ellie as she passed them and took her seat. Derek waived from the back as Rose continued talking to their friends and she also spotted Kenny and Sidney sat in the middle deep in conversation with each other.

Jen boarded the coach last, she looked tired as she walked up the coach to do a head count before they set off. She stopped at Kate and smiled

"Are your mother and aunt not going on this trip too?" she asked

"No, they were feeling energetic and have decided to go on the bike tour around the vineyards today" explained Kate

"Oh no, I hope they don't have a repeat of the gin tour! They will never get the bike back down to the port" Jen laughed as she left to continue her head count.

As they left the port and headed towards Segesta, Maria took up the microphone and spoke to them about the surrounding area

"You see on the right there are salt flats, Sicily is famous for its sea salt and ships it all over the world. If you look to the left you will see mounds of salt waiting to be shipped."

Maria discussed salt at length for the next 20 minutes of the journey. She switched briefly to wine when they passed a large vineyard on the road and then went straight back to salt. They were saved from Maria discussing the chemical components of sea salt by their arrival at the hillside road that led to the archaeological site and the temple of Aphrodite. Maria then instructed them that the coach would drop us at the café and gift shop and we were to walk the remaining distance to the amphitheatre and dig site further up the hill.

When they got off the coach Kate said "Do you know what was missing from that journey? She never mentioned the salt. You would think that they would say something about it considering Sicily is known for it"

It was a sweltering heat as they took to the rocky hillside path, Kate steadied herself on Ellie as they all made their way to the top of the hill. At the summit Maria pointed out the Corleone hills in the distance. Ellie took a few pictures, it was beautiful. The green hills sloped down to the Mediterranean Sea, there were goats grazing on a nearby hilltop.

Maria then took them around the dig site explaining all the different artefacts that had been found. They were led through the pathways until they arrived at the amphitheatre built into the hillside. It was breath-taking, the performance area was lit by the afternoon sun and the audience were able to enjoy whatever performance would have been acted out with the beautiful backdrop of the hills and sea as the stage.

Kate was enjoying the scenery and the sun as she sat on the stone seats and took it all in. She noticed Kenny and Sydney were in a loving embrace as they sat on the row in front of them. Kate smiled as she covertly watched their tender interactions. There was a deep love between them that she had long realised that she felt for Ellie. She sighed as she let her mind wander to her potential future with Ellie, the two of them returning here in 40 years' time to reminisce on their life together. Kate could no longer imagine a future that didn't have Ellie in it. The worry she had that they were moving too fast had long gone. She wanted that future with Ellie and at this moment she was formulating a plan to propose to the woman she loved.

They re-joined the group and headed back down the path towards the café where they spent some time eating lunch and sunning themselves at a picnic table.

Maria was now directing anyone who wished to see the temple to follow her. They all got up and started the long trek up the steep gravelly hill, the path had large steps and was very uneven. They took their time but even Ellie had to admit that she was exhausted after the trek up but once they saw the site at the top, the exhaustion was forgotten. The temple was built and designed by the Greek architects that built the Parthenon and was in fact very similar in design. Maria went on to explain that it was built to withstand earthquakes due to the different types of stone used in the construction. The temple was never finished so you could see the different shades of stone in the pillars. There is a very active volcano in the area and this temple has withstood several eruptions and countless earthquakes throughout the centuries without ever sustaining any damage.

As they were about to leave, Ellie walked to the foot of the temple and picked up a small piece of rock. She handed it to Kate as a memento of the temple.

Finally at the bottom of the hill again they were allowed some time to shop in the gift shop before boarding the coach once more. Kate and Ellie only bought water as they were hot from being in the sun all day. Kate had a burnt nose and Ellie was scarlet with sunburn on her arms and legs.

The journey back to port was fast but it didn't stop Maria continuing her history of salt through the ages.

"Seriously, how much does she love the salt? Does she have shares in it or something?" whispered Ellie as Kate snorted a laugh. When they arrived back at the docks they asked the ship staff if the cycling tour had returned yet. They were told that it was due in anytime now so Kate and Ellie walked hand in hand along the portside to wait for the cyclists return. They were admiring a statue of Garibaldi when the cycling tour started arriving. They were looking for Aggie or Peggy but couldn't see them and started to worry.

"You don't think they had an accident do you?" asked a worried Kate

"No they probably are just a bit slower, don't worry they should be here any minute" soothed Ellie.

No sooner had she said that than a police car drove down the hill and stopped at the dock. The officer got out and opened the back door of the car and out poured Aggie with Peggy landing on top of her.

"Oh no, what have they done now?!" said an exasperated Ellie as she ran up to the car to help scoop the delinquents from the ground as a very irate Sicilian police officer was shouting at them and pointing at his car.

"What the hell is going on?" asked Ellie as she lifted a giggling Peggy from the ground.

"Ellie!! Thish man seems a bit miffed at ush" slurred Peggy

"He seems to think that we've hit his car on purpose" said an indignant Aggie as she hiccupped her way to her feet unsteadily.

Ellie turned to the irate officer and tried to calm him down

"What happened sir?"

"These crazy women hit me with their bike Senora!" he explained in broken English.

He pointed to the side of the car and the large dent in the door before he opened the boot and hauled out the tandem bike with a mangled front wheel.

"They drunk in charge of this...this..."

"Bike young man, it's a bike" muttered Aggie, who had resumed a seated position on the ground as Peggy snorted a laugh

"Aggie" warned Ellie with a glare as she made a zip movement over her mouth

"Sir I apologise, I'll take responsibility for these women and any damage that they have inflicted. I'm an Inspector with the Scottish Police service and I will take custody of them if that is agreeable with you?" Ellie tried the professional route while trying to ignore Peggy as she staggered into her and started hugging her.

"Ellie I love you, yer a wee cracker. Can you gies a wee haun back to the ship? The world seems to be moving"

Kate had been standing by her mother listening and trying to let Ellie handle this but she couldn't stay quiet any longer. She walked up to the Italian police officer and smiled at him.

"Sir, I will happily pay for the damage to your car right now. I'll happily write a cheque to cover the damage and I'll even add an additional 500 euros for you as a donation towards the local police department with my gratitude" she kept smiling at him as she took his arm and led him to the driver's side of his car.

"No, no it's ok Senora, local garages fix police cars for free. There is no need. Please just get these crazy women on their ship and away from here. Please" he begged as he watched Ellie grabbing both of them and leading them unsteadily back to the docks. Kate didn't wait around for him to change his mind; she grabbed the mangled tandem and kissed him quickly on the cheek

"Grazie" she smiled at him as she turned to follow her delinquent family and he sheepishly waved back at her.

When they reached the boat they saw Jen who was waiting to check in the last of the straggling passengers. She took one look at Ellie and rolled her eyes as she ran forward to help her.

"Not again! How could they possibly have got drunk on a bike ride?" she asked as she took hold of Aggie and started carry-dragging her up the gangway into the ship

"Don't ask me, they are professional trouble makers these two. They've knackered the bike they were on and nearly got arrested for criminal damage if Kate hadn't managed to charm the local police into letting them go. Honestly what am I getting myself into with this family" she joked as she felt a little bit of drool leave Peggy's mouth and run down her neck.

They managed to get them back to their cabin to sleep it off again while Kate went to reception to pay for the damage to the bike and offer her apologies for their behaviour. Apparently the cycle instructor was still in shock in the staff canteen.

CHAPTER 17

◆ ◆ ◆

As Aggie and Peggy were in no condition for dinner, Ellie and Kate decided to go themselves. They went up to the observation deck and watched the sunset as Ellie wrapped her arms round Kate from behind. It was a perfect moment and neither of them spoke as they watched the sun disappear behind the horizon as a warm gust of wind whipped their hair around them.

They had dinner in the Chinese restaurant on deck 7 and watched small fishing boats slowly making their way out to sea as they ate. Ellie was watching Kate as she ate her meal and wished she already had the ring she was planning to give Kate. This would have been a perfect time she thought. She wanted to do it properly though so she would wait until she had the ring sorted first.

At the same time Kate was deep in thought, this was a perfect moment to ask the question but she really wanted to go give Ellie her grandmother's ring. It was important to her. She would bide her time, they had time to get this right.

After dinner they strolled along the deck and chatted, laughed about the antics of the day and enjoyed their time alone together. They heard raucous laughter and yelling coming from the bar at the end of the deck so peeked in to see what the commotion was all about. The Queen was dancing on top of a table with a drink in her hand as she was surrounded by equally drunk passengers singing along to 'grease lightening'. Ellie and Kate stood watching this show for a few moments until the song changed to 'Beautiful Sunday' and every Scottish woman in the bar screamed in delight and rushed to the dancefloor. The Queen and Queen mother were among the first to get there and, en masse, they started to do the slosh.

"I'll never understand why every Scottish woman reacts this way to the slosh. It's like a calling beacon. Every one of them gets up for the slosh." Ellie remarked as she turned towards Kate and realised she was no longer by her side. She panicked and looked around until she finally found Kate on the dancefloor, also dancing to the slosh.

"Like I said, every Scottish woman" Ellie muttered as she watched the antics from the edge of the dancefloor. She had lost Kate for the duration of the song so she enjoyed watching her free and happy for a while. Her phone rang after a few minutes and she saw that it was Gavin trying to reach her; she stepped back out on to the quiet of the deck to take the video call.

"Gavin, where have you been? I've been trying to get in touch for ages"

"Sorry boss lady, I've been in court giving evidence at a trial that was brought forward so I've had my phone off most of the time. It's took me a bit of time to track down the information you wanted but I've got something for you. Mary Rankin got married in Troon in 1978 to a Jack Reid. She took his name from then on and also started to use her middle name on any official documents. She has been Elizabeth Reid since then. She has two children, a boy and a girl. I'm still working on their information for you. Elizabeth Reid is still alive and still lives in Troon. Her husband died a few years ago, he was a local businessman and get this, his will leaves her a tidy sum of £750,000 so she's well off but there is only one child remembered in the will. He left his son £50,000 and his business in the will but nothing for the daughter."

"This is great Gavin; do you have the kids names? I'm trying to check if they are possibly on board."

"I don't have the daughter's info yet but the son mentioned in the will is called Kenneth Reid. Does that help?"

"Possibly, there's a Kenny on board that fits the age range. I'll have to have a chat with him I think. How's court going?"

"It's good so far, Anderson's lawyer is going down the diminished responsibility route but there's no way that's going to wash. We have the evidence that he had been poisoning his mother for months before giving her that fatal dose. I doubt the trial will be lengthy if I'm honest. How is your holiday going? And what is that noise? Is that the slosh going on behind you?" he asked excitedly

"Oh god, not you too! Honestly that dance is like Scottish hypnosis. I've already lost Kate to it tonight as it is"

"Kate's dancing? Lemmie see!" grinned Gavin. Ellie turned the camera round and showed Gavin the love of her life currently having a right old knees-up.

"Brilliant, sea air seems to agree with her. Good for her, oh and tell her congratulations again on the book award. There's a public vote section so everyone at the station has been voting for her in droves. In fact the Internet crime division has devised a way to block vote hundreds at a time and they are going to.."

"No, no way. Tell them not to do that. Kate would be devastated if she won that way. She will win it on the merit of her book, she won't need that." Said Ellie confidently.

"Ok, if you're sure. I'll tell them to knock it on the head. Just tell her we are all routing for her and send her my love will you?"

"Of course I will, she will be happy to know you lot are behind her. I think she's still a little shocked by the nomination."

"Hang on, how come I don't see the beauty of Aggie and Peggy cutting up the dancefloor? It's not like them to miss a party" Gavin asked with concern. Ellie then had to explain the cycle ride of death to him as Gavin had tears streaming down his face as he belly laughed through the story.

"Oh god I love those two, I wish you had got that on camera" he said breathlessly as he wiped tears from his eyes. "Aren't you glad they will soon be your in laws"

"Shhh, not so loud Gav! Jesus, Kate is just in there she could have heard you."

"Nah, there's still another minute of the song left so we're good until then. I picked up the ring from the jewellers as requested. It looks old, where did you get it?"

"It's Kate's grandmother's ring. I asked Aggie for it a few weeks ago and had it resized. Kate was really close to her gran, she tells me stories about her all the time. I had thought about buying a new ring but this just felt right you know?"

"It's perfect Els, I'm excited for both of you. I'd better go now; I need to walk your babies before they settle in for the night. They are currently getting a bedtime story from the missus."

"You're joking!" Ellie laughed

"I wish I was mate honestly, she's lost her bloody mind over those pups. I may have adopted a westie for her though. A 2 year old called Angus, I've filled in all the paperwork so once we hand back your pups I can surprise her with our very own."

"That's sweet, say hello from me and I'll talk to you soon" Ellie hung up just as Kate came through from the bar out of breath but smiling.

"Was that Gavin?" she asked as she pecked Ellie sweetly on the lips and started to walk back to the cabin.

"It was, he sends his love and also to tell you that the entire station has been voting for you for the award. They're proud of you."

"Really? That's amazing; remind me to send in some cakes for them when I get home. Did he have any news for you on Mary Rankin?"

"He did, she's changed her name to Elizabeth Reid but get this; her son is called Kenneth Reid."

"Who's Kenneth Reid? I don't recognise that name" Kate asked as they walked along.

"I think he might be Kenny, the wee one from the couple that I met in Pompeii's brothel. I need to talk to him to find out."

"Do you think he's the Majors son?"

"I really don't know. Kenneth is the only child remembered in Jack Reid's will. I can't imagine him disinheriting his own flesh and blood and giving money to a step child. It doesn't make sense."

"If that's the case, I don't see how he has any motive to kill the Major. He's not done anything to him." Kate responded.

"I know, but I need to ask him. Sometimes motive is not as clear to an outsider. For all we know he loves his sister and wants revenge on her behalf or something." Ellie said not really believing it herself but she knows better than to discount a lead before knowing the facts.

"I'll drop you off at the cabin and then I'll go looking for him."

"No you won't, if it's just you, it will feel like an interrogation.

Bring me with you and its two couples chatting. I'll talk to Kenny's husband while you find out what you need to know." At that Kate dragged Ellie back inside and started looking in all the bars for Kenny.

They finally found them listening to jazz in the small lounge at the back of the ship. There were few others in the lounge and it was made very cosy by the candles lit on each table. Kenny spotted them and waived over for them to join the table.

"Well hello ladies, would you like to join us? I'll get you both a drink. What will it be?" asked Sidney kindly as he held the chair open for Kate.

"Just coffee for me thanks" replied Ellie as she sat down beside Kenny.

"Sidney I'll help you with the drinks, I'm not sure what I would like." Said Kate as she escorted him to the bar smiling at Ellie. Good thinking Kate thought Ellie as she turned to Kenny. She decided against the softly softly approach and asked the direct question in the hopes that it would shock him into honesty.

"Kenny can I ask you something? Is your surname Reid?"

"It was before I married Sidney. How did you know?" he asked with surprise.

"Well I don't know if you are aware but I'm looking in to the death of the Major. I've found out a few things about him and I need to ask you about your family life. Is your mother Elizabeth Reid?"

"Y..y..yes she is; what do you want to know about her for?" Kenny asked defensively, anger flashing in his eyes.

"Cards on the table? Elizabeth Reid had a child out of wedlock and the father left before the baby was born. The father of the child was the Major. Now the Major was murdered, very cleverly, by someone who knew enough about him to find his weakness. I need to ask you Kenny, did you kill him for your mother?"

"Her? You must be joking! That woman hasn't been my mother for over 25 years!" he said angrily with tears forming in his eyes. He took a breath and calmed himself.

"My mother kicked me out of my home when I was 16. I told her I was gay and she kicked me out with nothing but the clothes on my back. I've not spoken to her since. My dad was a lovely and kind man, he helped me out in secret by setting me up with a flat and got me a job in the office. He even met Sidney towards the end of his life. He left me money and the business when he died and my mother tried to contest the will. She's poison; I didn't know the Major was my sisters real father. To be honest, I don't think she even cares about that. She is happy and lives in New York. I wouldn't do anything for my mother, believe me, killing someone who wronged her is a gay cliché that even I wouldn't touch" he smiled a little. "Do you need my alibi for whenever he was killed?"

"It would help" responded Ellie quietly

"Let's see, we were out seeing the sights during the gin tour and then we got back to the ship and went straight for dinner. We then went to the theatre show and then joined in the late quiz in the lounge. We were with a large rowdy table of people until at least 1.30am and then we went back to our cabin. We met back up with some people the next morning at breakfast and then went off ship with them. Does that fill in enough for you?"

"It does, thank you. I just needed to check, I hope you don't mind."

"No it's fine honestly. I know you need to check everyone and I suppose I have a better link than most."

"One more question, is you mother on this cruise?"

"If she is I wouldn't recognise her I'm afraid, I was quite young when I left and I haven't seen her since. I doubt I could pick her out of a line-up" he admitted.

Sidney and Kate arrived with the drinks and they said no more about it. They enjoyed some idle chit chat as they drank but made their excuses to leave shortly after.

Back in the cabin she told Kate about the conversation as they got ready for bed. She listened thoughtfully and then said "I don't see him being a killer Ellie, I don't see his motive at all. Sure it's strange that he happens to be on this cruise but there's not actual link between the two men and he had no reason to resent the Major, his mother on the other hand sounds like a right piece of work"

"I know; I'm going to go to the Captain in the morning and ask him for the passenger list to see if there is an Elizabeth Reid on board. It's the only lead I've got left."

CHAPTER 18

◆ ◆ ◆

Ellie was at the Captain's office early the next morning and was waiting for him to arrive after the morning staff meeting.

"Ah good morning Ellie, how can I help you? How is the investigation going?" he said smiling at her as he took his seat across from her at the desk.

"Well I have a lead that I need to check up on. I think that the person who killed the Major did it because of something that happened in Northern Ireland in the 1970's. The Major was stationed over there during the Troubles and got involved with a local woman. The IRA didn't take kindly to this and started attacking the girl's family. The Major was sent back home for his own safety and the girl also left the province shortly after. I think that either the girl or one of her family members had killed the Major in revenge."

"After all this time? Why wait 40 years?" the Captain said incredulously

"I honestly think it's the first time there has been any contact with the Major since he left Belfast. I think this was a once in a lifetime shot for the killer and they took it." explained Ellie.

"What do you need from me? I assume you need information and that's why you're sat in my office so early rather than a desire for my charming company?" he joked as Ellie smiled and nodded.

"Very well, what can I get for you?"

"I need you to check the passenger list to see if there is a woman called Elizabeth Reid listed as a passenger."

"I can do that now; just give me a few moments to check the system." The Captain was clicking away at pages on his screen and typing for a few minutes before he had a result.

"Yes we have her on board. She is in a double cabin with her friend Bridget Connolly. There are a couple of our older passengers and they are in a cabin on deck 6."

Ellie was excited, she recognised the names but she wanted to make absolutely sure before she acted.

"Captain you took all of our pictures when we first boarded the ship, do you have a file with those pictures so that I can confirm her identity?"

"Of course, it's already attached to her account here" he turned the screen around for Ellie to see and it confirmed it at last; Elizabeth Reid as the Queen.

"Captain this next bit is important; can you tell when she booked her holiday? Was it before or after the Major?" Ellie asked, she needed to know if there was any premeditation.

The Captain wasted no time in tracking down the booking information for both of them. He quickly scanned through the booking confirmations and then shook his head.

"No she booked well in advance, almost a year ahead in fact whereas the Major only booked the cruise a month before as part of a discount sale we were having at that time."

"Thanks Captain, this is staring to make sense now."

"So Mrs Reid killed the Major?" he asked obviously shocked at the notion. "What do we do now?"

"We need to find proof, I only have a back story and conjecture to go on right now and I need to have something concrete to give to port authorities in Palma tomorrow or she will be able to leave without questioning. Would it be possible for me to conduct a search of her room?"

"Ordinarily I wouldn't permit it, but as there seems to be an urgency of time I'll give you my pass key and you can do a search. Please try to be discreet though Ellie. It would be difficult to explain to ladies if they happen to catch you snooping." warned the Captain.

"Not to worry, I've got a plan to make sure I'm not disturbed"

"I was afraid of that" joked the Captain as Ellie left the office.

Ellie returned to the cabin to find that not only was Kate dressed and ready for the day but that she also had two very ill looking visitors.

"Good morning you two, how are your heads this morning?" Ellie asked as she sat down on the bed.

"Don't Ellie please, we're mortified. Kate has just filled us in on what we got up to yesterday and I can't believe we almost got arrested! I'm never drinking again. That's it, I'm getting too old for these antics" groaned Aggie

"You speak for yourself, you're a long time dead Aggie. At least we've had some adventures" commented Peggy as she placed a cool cloth against her forehead.

"Well I'm glad that you seem up for adventure Peggy, I've got a job for you."

"A job? What kind of job?" asked Peggy wearily

"I'm going to be searching the Queen's room soon and I need you and Aggie to follow her and the Queen Mother to make sure they stay away from their cabin while I'm searching. Kate has a forensic mind so I'll need her with me to search the room."

"What will you be looking for?" asked Aggie who was now alert.

"I don't know" Ellie admitted "But there must me something in there that could tie her to the murder. She is the only person with enough of a motive to want to kill him. I need to find hard evidence or she will get away with murder."

They set off immediately. They needed to make sure that they weren't anywhere close before they attempted the search. Ellie scanned the breakfast buffet and found them both in the queue for bacon. She left Peggy and Aggie to watch them. Ellie and Kate ran back to deck 6 and unlocked the cabin. They needed to work quickly. Kate started going through all their gift bags, she searched all the things that they had purchased until she found the bag from the gin distillery. She recognised it as the same one her mum had returned with. Inside were two bottles of gin, she checked the ingredients and found that almonds were the main ingredient for flavour. Digging in the bag she came up with a crumpled receipt at the bottom, Kate scanned it quickly and noticed that they had purchased three bottles of the gin. Where did the other one go?

"Ellie, I've got a receipt for three bottles of almond gin but they only have two here."

"That's great, keep that safe for now and keep looking" said Ellie as she was searching drawers; she came across a journal in the bedside table. She started scanning the most recent entries. There was not much after the Major's murder other than some choice words about her but at the start of the cruise there were some very hurtful entries about her son Kenny and his husband and how she was disgusted by his being there. Well that confirms she recognised him. Ellie kept scanning the pages and came across a few pages in which she mentions arguing with the Major and how much she hated him for what he had done to her family. She even threatened him one evening and she seemed to enjoy the feeling it gave her.

As Ellie was flicking through the diary some loose pages folded in the back fell out. She picked them up and read them and couldn't believe what she had found.

"Kate, I've found the pages of the Major's diary! She took them because they are about her and how he recognised her, they had a row and she had threatened his life. This proves she had been in his room!"

Kate was going through a stack of books on the coffee table and noticed a copy of her most recent novel was at the bottom. She picked it up and opened it and a key dropped out from the pages.

"Ellie what's this key?" she asked as she handed it over to Ellie. "It's a pass key, look it's exactly the same as the one the Captain gave me, that must be how she got into the room."

"How on earth did she manage to get a key?" wondered Kate as she continued to look around.

"Eddie! I remember a few days before the murder that some of the bar staff were talking about how Eddie was frantic because he had lost his pass key. I bet she took his key from his cart while he was in one of the rooms. I think we have enough Kate. The gin receipt proves they bought almond gin, the key shows that she had access to his room to plant it there and the diary pages prove she was trying to cover her tracks as she had made threats towards him."

Ellie picked up the phone and dialled reception in order to be put through to the Captain as a matter of urgency. She waited a moment and then he was on the line.

"Captain, I've found some evidence that links her to the murder but I need to have you here to witness my removal of the items from the room to keep the chain of evidence intact. Can you please get here as soon as possible?"

The Captain was there within three minutes, he watched Ellie pick up each item and place them in the plastic hygiene bags from the bathroom and label each one. Ellie handed all of it to him for safekeeping before they left the room and made their way to his office. As they turned the corner Kate spotted the Queen Mother making her way to the cabin from the other direction and being tailed by Aggie. Aggie spotted her daughter up ahead and quickly withdrew from her surveillance now that she knew it was safe.

In the Captain's office, Ellie called Gavin and asked him to notify British police to be waiting for the ship at Palma. She discussed all the evidence with him and he agreed that there was enough there for an arrest warrant. He said he would liaise with local port authorities from his side and see if he can issue an international arrest warrant before the ship docked the next day.

Ellie and the Captain were pacing the office, they couldn't make a move without the arrest warrant in place as it would tip their hand. Gavin said he would be in touch as soon as he heard from the CPS. Eventually Ellie's pacing was making the Captain dizzy

"Ellie for God sake will you go and find something to do to keep your mind occupied for a while? If you continue to pace like that in my office I may have to throw you overboard"

Ellie stopped pacing and sighed "Fine, I'll go and fill the family in about what's happening. That should kill some time, but please get in touch if you get contacted about the warrant?"

"Of course I will, don't worry I'll call as soon as I get word" he said as he shooed her out of his office.

Ellie walked down the corridor from the Captains office and, ahead of her, she spotted that strange American couple walking quickly towards the stairs. She wondered why they were down on this deck. It wasn't a passenger deck and there was nothing down here of interest. She was still bothered by them so she sped up and attempted to follow them to see what they were up to. She tailed them up three flights of stairs and onto deck 7. She watched them as they slowed their pace and seemed much more relaxed than she had ever seen them. They were laughing and slapping each other on the back like footballers who've scored a goal. Ellie tried to get closer to hear what they were talking about but as she got closer, her path was blocked by Peggy emerging from an inside door.

"Ah Ellie how are you dear? I was just coming to look for you, Kate wanted to know if you wanted anything to eat. She actually said 'that woman is wasting away to nothing because she's too busy working to eat' so if you know what's good for you dear I would eat something to calm her down" Peggy took Ellie's arm and guided her back inside and away from the American couple who were now sitting on sun loungers with a duffel bag between them that she hadn't noticed them carrying. Damn she really wanted to know what they were up to!

Ellie was pushing food around her plate in the restaurant; she didn't have much of an appetite. She was watching the Queen across the room; she was smiling and chatting away to her friend. Ellie watched her eyes; the smile did not meet her eyes. Ellie shivered slightly; the woman had no warmth in her expressions. Ellie's phone started ringing, breaking her vigil, she snatched it up and once she had plugged earphones in, answered Gavin's video call.

"Well?" she asked without any preamble

"Hi Els, yes I'm fine thanks for asking. Yes my wife is doing fine too. The weather is a bit off today but it's to settle this evening..."

"Gav" growled Ellie

"Fine, no niceties it is then. You've got the warrant. Spanish harbour police will be at Palma to meet you and place Mrs Reid under arrest once your ship docks. They will then hand her over to Detectives Miller and Austin who are already on their way to the airport to catch the next flight."

"Brilliant, thanks Gavin I owe you big time for that. Now all I need to do is have a little chat with Mrs Reid and see if I can get her to admit the charge, just to seal the case"

"Good luck boss lady, and I expect a very large amount of Toblerone to be handed to me when you get back. See you in a couple of days Els" Gavin grinned as he hung up.

"We got the warrant" Ellie whispered to everyone at the table.

"Excellent, what do you need to do now honey?" asked Kate as she squeezed her hand.

"I need to talk to her; I want to see if I can get a confession out of her before I hand her over tomorrow. As much as we have the evidence to convict her, a confession would help with the jury. The public tend to get a bit squeamish when it comes to convicting little old ladies." said Ellie as she finally started to tuck into her food, suddenly ravenous.

"Well that's good to know" responded Aggie. Everyone looked at her "I don't mean.....oh you know what I mean" she blustered

"No I don't think we do dear sister, who are you planning to bump off when you hit little old lady-hood?" teased Peggy

"Don't tempt me Margaret" glared Aggie as Ellie choked on a mouthful of chips. Ellie looked up and realised that she had missed the Queen leaving the restaurant.

"Shit, where did she go?" she muttered as she cleared away her plate.

"Ellie calm down, we're at sea and she doesn't know that she is a suspect in a murder. She won't be far away. You go and find the Captain and go see her, we will head to the lounge for the movie quiz." Kate kissed her gently and then got up and herded her mother and aunt towards the door.

Ellie found the Captain talking to Derek and Rose outside the shops.

"Ah Ellie, just the girl we wanted to see." said Derek warmly. "I was hoping that you and your family would join us tonight for a little drink and get some pictures before we all say farewell. We won't take no for an answer young lady" he winked.

"Well we are going to the theatre tonight but I don't think we have any plans after that so we would love to Derek" she smiled warmly at him before turning to the Captain "Sir I need to talk to you if you wouldn't mind?"

The Captain caught what she was referring to and nodded, he excused himself while also trying to extricate his arm from Rose who appeared to have taken a shine to him. When they were out of earshot he whispered to her "you have impeccable timing Ellie, that woman has been touching me up at every opportunity since we set sail. In fact so has he. I take it that you have your warrant?"

"We do so I would like to talk to Mrs Reid now and I need you to be there as witness just to keep us right. Do you have someone available that could possibly stand guard over her cabin overnight? Just to make sure she doesn't try to do a runner"

"I can have our head of security Anna to sort that out, even if she puts a couple of people on as a shift. Just let us know if and when it would be needed."

"Thank you Captain, hopefully she is in her cabin and we don't need to play hide and seek all over this bloody ship." muttered

Ellie as they arrived at the cabin door. The Captain knocked the door and they waited briefly before the door was opened by the Queen Mother.

"Ah good morning Ms Connolly, we were wondering if Mrs Reid was in and if we could have a chat with her?" said the Captain with a polite smile on his face. Bridget Connolly looked at him and then at Ellie and her eyes narrowed briefly before she replied.

"She's in the bathroom at the moment but come in if you must, I'm going to the bar. I don't want to be here for this." She passed them and walked down the corridor without another word. Ellie and the Captain wordlessly walked into the cabin and took a seat on the couch and waited for Elizabeth Reid.

CHAPTER 19

◆ ◆ ◆

I f Elizabeth Reid was surprised at visitors sitting in her cabin, she did not show it except for a narrowing of her eyes. She looked at both of them as she walked past them and took a seat in the armchair across from them. She didn't say a word; she just sat looking at them, waiting for them to start.

"Mrs Reid I don't know if you have met Ellie McVey this week, she has been investigating the death of Major Charleston. She would like to talk to you about it." The Captain explained calmly but firmly. Elizabeth glared hard at both of them

"I don't see why this interfering girl has any business investigating or asking questions of us. Who are you to be asking us anything?" she said harshly.

"I'm sorry; I should probably have introduced myself properly. I'm Detective Inspector McVey with Police Scotland. I have full authority to investigate criminal activity when it occurs on British soil or a British ship in international waters. Now I would like to ask you some questions regarding the death of Major Charleston. You knew him didn't you?" Ellie serves her first volley.

"Why would you think I know him?" I'm on holiday with my

friend and I've never met anyone here before." She said defensively. Ellie saw the slight glint of fear in her eyes so she decided to push.

"Really? You don't know anyone? Not even Kenny?" Ellie let that question hang in the air for a second. Elizabeth went pale and then heat creeped up her neck as anger flushed her.

"I knew Kenneth Reid, a nice boy who was kind to his mother and went to church. I don't know that freak that prances around with a man old enough to be his father, it's disgusting." She spat. "Old enough to be his father? Oh I don't think that's accurate, I doubt Sidney is more than ten years older than Kenny. Besides, they're happy, isn't that enough?" Ellie asked gently

"Filth. My son died when he left at 16."

Ellie sighed in frustration; there was no reaching the maternal side of this woman.

"So you know Kenny. You know the Major too, I know you do. I've seen his military record, I know why he had to leave Northern Ireland in 1976 and I know that you are Belfast born and bred, despite your attempts to mask your accent. You're Mary Rankin of Belfast, you moved to Scotland heavily pregnant and unmarried with your family destroyed by terrorist reprisals. Stop me if I go wrong by the way." Elizabeth glared at her with pure hatred. Ellie carried on

"So you move to Troon and marry a good man, you settle down with your children and live a good life. Your husband died a few years ago and leaves money to your son in his will which you contest. Fast forward to when you arrive on this cruise and you spot Major Charleston for the first time in over 40 years. You argue with him outside my room and threaten him. He dismisses you so you plan your vengeance. You know about his allergies, you knew him well once and I doubt you forgot that part. The gin tour mentions almond gin and that gives you the idea, you buy some bottles of it and pour one bottle into a water jug to place in the Major's room. It would only be a matter of time before he took a drink of what he thought was water. One sip is all it would take for him to go into anaphylaxis."

"A great story, you should write that down and get a best seller out of it. A story is all you have though; you have no proof of any of this. How would I get in to his room? Everyone bought almond gin on that tour, it was the one we sampled and enjoyed at the end. Now if you will excuse me, I've heard enough and I would like you to leave." She got up and marched to the door.

"Yes everyone bought the gin, you bought three bottles of it did you not?" asked Ellie

"No I bought two, here I'll show you if it will shut you up" she grabbed the bag and thrust it at Ellie who looked at it with a small smile.

"Yes I can clearly see two bottles there but the thing is, I also have this" she pulled the receipt out of her pocket "The receipt from your bag that states you in fact bought three bottles of the gin. Where did the other bottle go?"

"You're trying to frame me, you just happen to find a receipt did you? How convenient. It's just like you people to be sneaky and lie"

That did it, 'you people' thought Ellie 'oh you mean us gay people'

"I can assure you this was found in your room, I have a witness who was there when it was found. But let's go back to your other question of how you would get into his room. During the search of your room we also found this" at this point Ellie produced the pass key. "Do you know what this is?"

"It's a key" Elizabeth responded sarcastically "or don't they teach that in Police training these days?"

"Yes you're correct it's a key, it's a pass key that staff members use to access any door on the ship. Can you tell me why this key was in your possession?"

"I don't know, maybe that stupid steward dropped it on the floor when he was cleaning."

"Oh he dropped it, and then it hopped up onto the table and hid itself in a book at the very bottom of a pile did it?" Ellie replied coolly "Stop lying to me, you stole Eddie's pass key and used it to gain entry to the Major's room to leave the water jug full of gin. You left a note for Eddie supposedly from the Major to make sure he didn't come into the room. You tore out the pages of the Major's diary that concerned you and you hid them in here to make sure you couldn't be implicated. Mrs Reid I have means, motive and opportunity. The CPS agreed with me, there is an arrest warrant out for you and they will be waiting at Palma to take you back to face trial for murder. This is your one chance to get your side of the story out." Ellie left it at that and waited for her to make the next move; she could see Elizabeth's mind was racing, trying to find a way out of this hole. Ellie held her breath as Elizabeth's shoulders finally slumped and she sagged back into the chair defeated. She chuckled slightly and shook her head.

"I loved that man so much, he was a handsome bugger back then in his uniform. My daddy warned me not to talk to soldiers, that the boys wouldn't take kindly to fraternising with the enemy as he put it. I was young and in love, I didn't care about the troubles or what the boys thought, I only cared about him. He took me dancing and we had lovely walks up Cavehill when he was off duty. Then I found out I was pregnant, I thought that he would be happy. I had it all planned out in my head, we would get married and to hell with what the IRA or my daddy thought. We would be a lovely family and would get the hell out of Belfast once Edward's tour was over." She sighed as memories overwhelmed her. "It didn't happen; Edward was terrified that I was pregnant. He offered to get me on a boat to England to get a termination. I couldn't do that; I wouldn't have been able to go to mass again! The fact that he even suggested it showed me that he didn't know me at all. We had a row and he told me that he couldn't marry me and would never, It would ruin his career you see." She smiled bitterly as tears started to fall.

"I told my daddy, I couldn't hide it anymore you see. He was so angry and scared. He went to the barracks to see Edward, I suppose it was his way of protecting my honour but Edward refused to see him, coward. I never saw Edward after that, he stopped calling and didn't reply to my letters. Then daddy heard from a friend that the IRA was out for blood, furious that I was going to have a Brit's baby. They had put out a threat on Edward, me and my family. Of course Edward was shipped out immediately once the threat had been made. Mum and Daddy wanted to get me over to my Aunt in Scotland but I didn't want to leave my family, I was scared of doing this on my own so I stayed....my family paid the price. My brother died in a car bomb, he was only 17 for Christ sake. My poor Daddy was dumped in the gutter in his bloody carpet slippers with a hole in his head and my mother, well she was lame for the rest of her life after they shot her." She paused and took a shaky breath as she composed herself.

"Mum sent me away before anything else could happen and I went to live with Aunt Mary. My daughter Lynda was born two months after that, she's never met Edward. I tried to find him after she was born, tracked him to Glasgow but he refused to acknowledge either me or his daughter. I hated him for that, I swore I would get him back for his cowardice one day.....and now I have. I bought the gin; the almonds were perfect for a nut allergy. I waited for the steward to pop in to one of the cabins, I noticed that he always left his key on the cleaning cart. I took the key and hid it in my book, I waited until I saw him leave his room and I let myself in and placed the water jug where he would see it. I remembered he always liked a glass of water before bed. I then used the ship's writing paper to scribble a quick note asking not to be disturbed and I slipped it on to the steward's cart on my way out of the room. I also moved his epi pens from beside his bed, I hid them in his wash bag in the bathroom so that he wouldn't find them in time." She looked up defiantly "I don't care if I go to prison, I have health problems that would make a life sentence very short."

She seemed to have exhausted herself in her story; she sat slumped in the chair looking very frail and tired. Ellie couldn't feel sorry for her though.

"Mrs Reid I don't understand you, family means a great deal to you, so much that you've killed the man who refused to acknowledge his daughter. Yet you spurn your only son for something that he can't change. Kenny is happy and in love, why can't you accept him? Be a better mother to him than the Major was a father to Lynda, there's still time to put that right" pleaded Ellie emphatically.

If Elizabeth heard what she said, she didn't acknowledge it. She just sat staring at her hands that were trembling slightly. After a few moments of silence she cleared her throat.

"What happens now? Is there a prison cell on this ship that I've to be locked up in?"

"No" said the Captain "you are to remain in this cabin until the ship docks in the morning. There will be officers waiting to take you back to the U.K."

Elizabeth nodded her understanding. Ellie and the Captain got up to leave and Elizabeth stopped her "I know you mean well, but some things are past fixing. Too much hurt festers and there's no way of healing it even if I wanted to." She turned her back and went to her bed to lie down as Ellie left the cabin.

There was an officer from ship security sitting outside already and the Captain gave him instructions to ensure the lady did not leave the cabin for any reason. Anything she needs will be brought to her cabin, I'll trust you to make any arrangements that are necessary."

CHAPTER 20

◆ ◆ ◆

Ellie returned to her cabin and slumped against the door after closing it. Kate watched her from the couch and opened her arms to her and Ellie gratefully melted into the embrace and sighed contentedly.

"Did you get her?" asked Kate as she kissed Ellie's forehead

"I got her, she made a full confession and she will be arrested when we dock. She is technically under house arrest in her cabin at the moment. I understand her anger, she had a hard life because of him but there is no justification for killing a man after 40 years." Ellie grew silent again as she settled into Kate's soothing touches.

"Are you up for tonight? The theatre?" Kate asked as she stroked Ellie's hair.

"Yeah I'll be fine, just going to have an hour to relax and then I'll be grand. Oh shit! I forgot, I sort of agreed that we would all meet up with Derek and Rose after the theatre. I totally forgot, sorry honey"

"That's ok, they are nice people.....strange but nice. I'll let you have a bit of sleep honey, I'll write some book notes and wake you in an hour?"

"Perfect" murmured Ellie, already half asleep.

That evening they found a table at the theatre, they got there early and were glad they did as the room filled up quickly with people taking their last chance of watching a show before disembarkation. Rose waved over from their table and then turned back round to snuggle into Derek. For the first time in days, their friends were not with them.

The show for the last night was a big production dedicated to favourite musicals and it was a great show to watch. Peggy was singing along to the Sound of Music, Kate was singing along to Grease and Aggie started crying over Les Mis. The show was a triumph and the performers received a roaring standing ovation from the entire audience. The head of entertainment on board jumped up on stage with a microphone.

"Ah ladies and gentlemen you will all be leaving us tomorrow morning, on behalf of the entertainment staff I hope you have enjoyed your time with us here on 'The Dream.' I would like to bring some people up on stage to say goodbye to you and I hope that you will give them a huge round of applause as your holiday has run smoothly because of their hard work. Ladies and Gentlemen the staff of the Dream!"

He waived his hands and dozens of staff members trouped forward from the back of the theatre smiling and waving flags. There were stewards, chefs, bar staff, cleaners, bridge staff, lounge singers, engine workers and everyone in between. The audience cheered and clapped in appreciation; Peggy wolf whistled.

Shortly after they were leaving the theatre and met up with Derek and Rose who escorted them to a table in the show lounge and ordered a round of drinks. The entertainment in the lounge was a singing duo belting out hits of the 60s to an appreciative and somewhat tipsy audience.

"Well now, I must say we've been on many cruises over the years; but I have to admit this one has been the most entertaining for us hasn't is Rose?" said Derek as he passed cocktails to Peggy, Aggie and Rose and then handed lemonade over to Ellie and Kate.

"Oh absolutely, I mean when do you ever get to go on a cruise and end up with dead people on board. Very thrilling, so is it true Ellie? Was he murdered? It's the rumour going around at the moment." asked Rose excitedly.

'Ah that's why we were invited for drinks' thought Ellie. 'Nosey gits' she looked around and saw Kate staring at them in disbelief, it was obvious she was having a similar inner monologue going on. Ellie decided there was no point in being evasive.

"Yes I'm afraid he was, I've been looking into his death for the last few days."

"Really? Oh how exciting!! Do you have any clues? How did it happen?" Rose was now perched at the end of her chair, full attention centred on Ellie.

"I won't be able to tell you everything as it's still a police investigation" Ellie said cagily "but I can tell you that the Major was murdered via a bottle of gin. The gin contained almonds and the Major had a severe nut allergy. He also detested gin so there is no way he would have chosen to drink it so it was put in a water jug."

"Seriously? How ingenious. Hold on, how did he not smell the alcohol? I mean if he was expecting to drink water, surely he would have got a whiff of alcohol from the glass?" asked Derek with his brow furrowed. It was Kate who answered this question.

"Usually yes you would smell it, but the Major was never seen without a glass of wine in his hand. All he did was drink red wine, the alcohol would have already been on his breath and in his nose beforehand. I doubt he would have noticed the subtle smell given off by that gin."

"Really ladies it's too ingenious" remarked Derek. "Do you know who did it yet? You're a clever lady Ellie so I'm sure you have suspicions"

"Actually yes, I've spoke to someone who has confessed to the murder. They will be arrested tomorrow at Palma. I'm afraid I can't tell you any more about them so please don't ask me"

"Oh no we won't, don't worry. Well congratulations Ellie, this must have been like a busman's holiday for you having to investigate instead of relaxing and getting a tan" said Rose as she started on her second cocktail.

"It was, hopefully I don't end up making a habit of it" she joked. Ellie noticed that Aggie was a little quiet, she looked over to find her deep in conversation with Derek. He was leaning in awfully close and kept laughing at whatever Aggie was talking about. Ellie kicked Kate under the table and directed her attention to the horror before them. Kate's eyes widened in panic and she leaned in to Ellie and whispered harshly

"What the hell are we going to do? I don't think mum has realised that she's being lined up as the swingers next victim!"

Ellie had an idea; she excused herself from the table and walked towards the stage where the duo were taking a water break. She spoke briefly to them and they nodded their heads and smiled. Kate was watching in confusion while her panic continued to rise as Derek was now wrapping his arm around an oblivious Aggie. Ellie returned and winked at Kate before whispering "don't worry I have a plan to get your mum away from the table for a few minutes."

"How are you going to do that?" Kate asked confused. She didn't have long to wait to find out, the band were back on stage and the singer spoke into the microphone.

"We've had a request for all the Scottish women tonight, we hope you enjoy this." They started playing 'Beautiful Sunday' and sure enough, Aggie's eyes lit up "Peggy get up! It's the slosh!" she jumped up, knocking Derek's arm away as she went and hauled her sister to the dancefloor and started dancing the slosh. Ellie was grinning and Kate rolled her eyes and shook her head.

"Yes fine! I know! All Scottish women dance to this song. Don't look too smug though Ellie or I'll get them to play Whigfield's Saturday Night."

They managed to say their farewells to Derek and Rose just before 11pm, Derek appeared to admit defeat in the attempt to woo Aggie and the conversation for the rest of the evening was light and funny. They took plenty of pictures as a reminder of a great holiday and then everyone took turns at running up and down to the dancefloor whenever a tune they loved was played. The band started to play an old Glenn Miller number and all the couples took to the dancefloor for a last romantic dance. Kate took Ellie's hand and pulled her towards the dancefloor, Ellie was nervous as she really really could not dance…at all….she had a habit of falling or tripping and on one occasion, punching someone in the mouth during a very enthusiastic hand wave. Kate didn't care and pulled her close as they swayed in the middle of the dancefloor. Kate didn't want any fancy moves; she just wanted the closeness to Ellie that the dance would bring. She wrapped her arms around Ellie's waist and moved the two of them gently. She looked up and found Ellie gazing at her softly with a smile.

"See I knew you could dance" teased Kate

"I'm literally swaying to music honey; it's hardly strictly is it?"

"Well it's enough for me" said Kate contentedly as she placed her head on Ellie's shoulder and they lost themselves in the music just swaying in each other's arms.

"I love you Kate" whispered Ellie

"I love you too"

The next morning was chaos, staff were carrying passengers' luggage off the ship to be picked up inside the port. Everywhere you looked there were passengers sleepily emerging from their cabins and trying to either grab a quick breakfast or to make their way down to the disembarkation area. There were queues at every lift; Ellie and Kate decided to walk down. They met Peggy and Aggie waiting at the gangway ready to go, Peggy's eyes were darting all over the place as if she was looking for someone.

As they made their way down to the dock Kate elbowed Ellie and pointed ahead of them. Elizabeth Reid was being escorted into a police car parked on the dock, her friend Bridget watched from a distance but then turned and walked away.

They made their way along the dock towards the port terminal, Ellie looked around and noticed that there were still several police officers milling around in dark uniforms scanning the faces of everyone leaving the ship. Ellie was about to comment on it when Peggy rushed forward, barging her out of the way. This appeared to be a signal to the police officers as they all started running towards where Peggy was now grappling someone and joined in the tussle.

"Has she gone completely around the bloody twist?!" screamed Aggie in shock. Ellie was about to run and help but then the crowd of police parted and Peggy walked forward dragging someone in handcuffs with her as a large police officer was behind her dragging a similarly clothed person with him also in handcuffs. Peggy stopped and spoke to a man in a sharp suit that had appeared from a silver Audi parked nearby. He smiled and shook her hand before taking the prisoners off her hands and bundling them into the car. It was the American couple that had been arrested. Ellie and Kate stood dumbfounded.

Peggy dusted herself off and smiled at them before ushering them away from the main terminal and towards a private room.

"Peggy what the hell is going on?" asked Ellie once they were in a small office and seated on a leather couch by the wall. There was two way glass on the opposite wall and they watched the rest of the passengers that were queueing up for their luggage and getting called forward for the coaches to take them to the airport. Peggy was watching people for a few moments and then turned back to Ellie.

"Those people that were arrested, the Americans that you found suspicious?" Ellie nodded and Peggy continued "They are members of a right-wing terrorist group based in Virginia called the hand of God. MI6 and homeland security have been monitoring their movements for years. They have been planning attacks on liberal targets throughout Europe and their aim is to start a race and religion war, the world is on a knife edge already what with Trump, Brexit and the resurgence of right-wing politics throughout Europe. They needed funds, specifically they needed large amounts of untraceable cash in order to pay for the weapons they will need to start this chaos.

"Don't tell me they planned a terrorist attack on the ship?!" said Aggie clutching her throat in panic.

"Oh don't be so dramatic Aggie dear, do you think I would have had us all on a cruise ship if I thought they were going to blow it to smithereens?" Peggy tutted with impatience.

"This is all to do with money. The group have planted various agents on cruise ships all over the world, they all seem to be on the ships just when the crew's wages are to be paid. Many of the ships still pay in cash as it is easier than having to deal with bank accounts from all over the world, the crew are from dozens of different countries, some don't have bank accounts at all so cash is the easiest means of payment. Two nights ago our surveillance caught them breaking in to the pursers safe where they stole over $200,000 in American currency. It was the evidence we needed to pick them up once they docked. Hopefully they will provide intel on the group now that they are heading for a lengthy prison sentence."

"This was why we were on the cruise? So that you could observe them without being suspected?" asked Kate

"Of course, they would have seen me as some old codger with a pending drink problem if they were to have watched me at all during the trip. It was the perfect cover so I made up the story about winning the cruise, it was the only way I was sure that you all would come at short notice. I even made sure that your case load got quiet just around that time Ellie so that there was nothing to keep you home."

"Peggy you are a frightening woman do you know that?"

"It's been said" she laughed "just keep on my good side" she warned with a wink.

CHAPTER 21

◆ ◆ ◆

Ellie was running around the flat trying to tidy as quickly as she could. Kate was out at the awards dinner that she had been nominated for best fiction novel. Aggie had accompanied her and they had both left earlier in the evening in beautiful evening dresses with matching bags, Peggy had got her friend Tanya round to do their makeup professionally. Ellie was varying out her plan tonight and she was nervous as hell.

She looked around, the living room was spotless and candles twinkled on every surface. The dogs had grudgingly had a bath and were now white and fluffy and sleeping in their beds by the fireplace. The dining table was set with candles and a bouquet of sunflowers which were Kate's favourite flower.

"Ding dong! Ellie are you here?" called Peggy as she came through the door with Gavin carrying covered dishes.

"Peggy you're a legend thank you so much for doing this" Ellie exclaimed as she helped deposit the dishes in the kitchen.

"Hey! What about me I helped too!" grumbled an indignant Gavin with a pouted lip.

"Young man you helped carry two dishes approximately 10 feet from the car, I've been cooking these all day so let me have the plaudits" glared Peggy as Gavin gulped and backed away from the woman slowly.

"What are we having?" asked Ellie as she uncovered some of the dishes.

"I've made sweet potato curry with pilau rice and some home-made naan bread for your main course followed by cardamom mousse. I also have brought schloer for the drink because I refuse to have this moment toasted by two cans of coke!"

"Oh yeah, that's a good point actually. I'm glad you thought of it."

"Are you nervous?" asked Gavin excitedly

"I've never been so scared in my life mate, my hands are shaking" replied Ellie

"Nothing to be worried about Ellie; tonight will go as planned so stop stressing. Now is there anything else that needs to be done?" asked Peggy as she looked around.

"I think I'm all set now."

"Ok, so now we wait" said Peggy.

Kate was fiddling with her water glass as she listened to the acceptance speech of Oisin Harkins who had just won the rising star in poetry. Aggie touched her wrist gently.

"Are you nervous Katie?"

"No, not really, I don't expect to win the award so I'm just working on my gracious loser smile and clap" Kate joked.

"Why don't you think you will win? You have a best seller Katie; you have just as much chance as the others." Aggie's protective parent mode had been activated.

"That's true but I don't do anywhere near the amount of promotion that some of the others do. You see that woman sitting over there in the blue dress?" she pointed to a tall woman holding court at a table closer to the stage. "She has been on Loose Women, Lorraine Kelly and This Morning within the last two weeks. I don't really do much of that, I would rather be writing than talking about it so I kind of suffer in that respect I would say." She admitted.

"Bollocks" responded Aggie

"Mum!" said a shocked Kate

"No it's bollocks Katie, a good book is a good book. It doesn't matter that you aren't on tv every five minutes. This award is based on the book. Oh wait shhh your award is up next."

"And now we've come to the award for best crime novel. Voting for this award is split between the judges and a public vote. The 2020 award for crime fiction goes to...."

Ellie, Peggy and Gavin were watching the live online feed of the awards ceremony. They were just about to announce the fiction winner. Peggy was holding on to Gavin like he was a life vest on a sinking ship. Ellie's leg was jumping with nerves.

"..the winner is.....Katherine Mitchell!"

"Oh my God she did it!!" Peggy was crying and hugging, well choking, Gavin and Ellie sat still with tears running down her face as she watched the love of her life walk slowly up to the stage to receive her award.

Kate looked beautiful in a lilac dress and her auburn hair had been pinned in an elegant knot at the base of her neck. She looked shocked and was trying to compose herself while the applause settled down.

"Um....wow ok....I'm afraid as a writer I've let myself down this evening. I didn't write an acceptance speech." Laughter filled the room as she giggled nervously.

"I would like to thank my publisher and Editor Jan and Sarah for pushing me and getting the best out of every story. I want to thank my mum who is here with me this evening, hello mum" the camera pans to Aggie who is standing clapping and crying.

"I would also like to thank my Aunt Peggy for her constant support...and finally I would like to thank the person that fills my life with joy every day. Ellie I love you and this award is for you. Thank you." Kate was then escorted off stage to rapturous applause.

CHAPTER 22

◆ ◆ ◆

Kate walked through the door of the flat to find the living room dark except for candles. Aggie was behind her holding the award like it was the most precious thing in the world. As Kate walked further into the room a huge cheer erupted as Ellie, Peggy and Gavin sprang from the kitchen with champagne and schloer at the ready. The dogs were wakened by the noise and Bruiser started to bounce around them and bark his head off. Bella lifted her head and grumbled before going back to sleep with a huge sigh. Ellie was the first to reach Kate and she swung her round in her arms and then held her close.

"I'm so proud of you honey. It's well deserved and I have no doubt it's going to be the first of many. I love you" she kissed her soundly before she was barged out of the way unceremoniously by Peggy who wrapped her niece in a huge rib cracking bear hug.

"Oh my Katie, well done, oh I can't believe it" Peggy sobbed into Kate's hair as she continued the hug.

"Aunt Peggy....I kind of need to breathe..." she gasped as Peggy let her go at last.

Peggy composed herself and then looped her arm in Kate's "come into the kitchen Katie we have a celebration dinner made for you. It's your favourite sweet potato curry"

"Brilliant, thanks Peggy. The dinner at the awards thing was tiny, I'm so hungry. Now I know why mum stopped me running into the kebab shop"

Aggie had taken Ellie to the side "Ellie, are you ready?" she asked seriously studying the younger woman.

"I am; I've never been more ready." She said confidently.

"Good, let's do this" Aggie grinned.

Dinner was a rowdy affair; laughter filled the kitchen as Peggy regaled Gavin with stories of their antics on the cruise. Gavin nearly fell off the chair laughing at the tandem bike crash story. Aggie and Ellie cleared the desert plates away and switched the coffee maker on. Aggie subtly filled champagne flutes and then took her seat. She nudged Peggy to shut her up and the room fell silent. Kate was still laughing at the story Peggy had been telling when she looked around and saw that everyone was looking at her smiling.

"What? What's wrong? Have I got mousse on my face?" she began wiping her face with a napkin and then she felt Ellie take her hand. She turned to find Ellie standing beside her looking at her with such love in her eyes that it took Kate's breath away. "Ellie?" she whispered.

Ellie put her hand in her pocket and pulled out a small velvet box. She lowered herself on to one knee, never breaking eye contact with Kate, and opened the box to reveal a simple gold ring with an elegant diamond set in the middle.

"Kate? Will you..." Ellie was interrupted by a loud crash. Bruiser came running in from the living room with a pear in his mouth. He had obviously decided he wanted some fruit from the bowl on the coffee table and had toppled it over.

"Perfect timing little man" grumbled Ellie as Bruiser ditched the pair and jumped into her lap to give her slobbery kisses. Kate was laughing and crying at the same time. She got down on the floor with Ellie and lifted the box. She looked at Ellie and smiled. "Ask me" she said quietly as she picked Bruiser up and handed him over to Gavin.

"Kate...I love you...will you marry me?"

"Yes of course I will" Kate beamed as Ellie finally took a breath and shakily placed the ring on Kate's finger. Kate looked at the ring and recognition dawned immediately.

"Gran's ring? How did you?"

"Your mum gave it to me and I got it resized for you." Ellie explained as she ran her finger over the ring.

"Ellie you have no idea..." Kate choked up a little "I asked mum for this ring when we got back from the cruise. I was planning on proposing to you with it. But mum said that she couldn't find it." Kate was now crying and realised they were still on the floor and that the room was still quiet around them. She looked around as Ellie helped her up and realised that Gavin was crying on Peggy's shoulder as she patted his back in a soothing manner and Aggie was still sitting smiling as if everything in her life was perfect.

Once Gavin had composed himself he ran over to congratulate the couple, his tears ran again when Ellie said he could be best man. Aggie hugged her daughter tightly and whispered "you've got a good one there Katie, she is going to make you very happy" and then she turned to Ellie, her soon to be daughter in law and hugged her as tightly as she could, trying to convey her love for the woman who has made her daughter happy.

EPILOGUE

◆ ◆ ◆

Elizabeth Reid's trial was held a few months after they got back from the cruise. She pled not guilty and the trail lasted a few weeks. Ellie and Kate were both summoned to testify for the prosecution. The Captain provided the information he had at the witness box too.

Ellie noticed that Kenny and Sidney were in the public gallery every day of the trial. They sat beside a woman who couldn't have been anything but Kenny's sister. The Jury retired and took only six hours to unanimously find Elizabeth Reid guilty of the murder of Major Edward Charleston.

During sentencing the Judge took in to account her age and a crime free life up until this point. Mrs Reid's doctor gave evidence of her medical issues that included heart disease and lung disease. The Judge still thought that the calculated manner of the murder showed a woman who still had her faculties and therefore still thought a custodial sentence was the best course of action. He sentenced her to the lowest sentence that he could hand her under the letter of the law and Elizabeth Reid was imprisoned for 15 years with the possibility of parole in 6 years. She was then taken to Cornton Vale prison to carry out her sentence.

Elizabeth showed no emotion as she was led from the dock, even when her daughter cried out for her from the gallery.

The Major's will was read after his body was finally released for burial. He left the entirety of his estate to the daughter that he had ignored in life. That must have been his way of making amends for his absenteeism for her entire life.

Derek and Rose kept in touch regularly after the cruise, they had invited Aggie down for a party they were throwing for 'like-minded souls' and Kate nearly had to beg her mother not to go and explained (again) what they meant by 'like-minded'.

Since Kate won the award she was in much demand for tv shows and had already appeared on breakfast tv to chat about her number 1 bestseller and the new book she was working on. She was also invited to be part of the Glasgow Arts Council and she jumped at the chance to be a part of it.

Ellie was given a commendation by the Chief Constable for her work on the Major's murder. Her leadership of the Serious Crimes Division was getting noticed by the powers that be, but she had no plans for climbing the ladder into a non-investigative role. She was happiest when she had a puzzle to work out; she returned to work to listen to Gavin whine about his new dog.

"Els it's not fair! I rescued the little bugger but who does he love? The wife! What do I get? He pees in my shoes, bites my ankles and growls if I even try to go near her. I'm telling you the dog is possessed!"

Peggy told Ellie in confidence that she had been promoted, although couldn't actually tell her what she was promoted to as it was highly classified. Aggie now spent every waking moment pouring over wedding magazines and calling her daughter constantly to discuss dresses and venues. Ellie avoided these calls like the plague, all she wanted to do was turn up, get hitched and get out of there.

Kate and Ellie when they got a moment to themselves would discuss what they would like for their wedding day, they were in no hurry. They were enjoying being an engaged couple for now.

The End

Printed in Great Britain
by Amazon

54463746R00097